MOONBORN

MARINA FINLAYSON

FINESSE SOLUTIONS

Cover design by Wicked Good Book Covers
Editing by Larks & Katydids
Formatting by Polgarus Studio

Published by Finesse Solutions Pty Ltd
2016/2/#01

Author's note: This book was written and produced in Australia and uses British/Australian spelling conventions, such as "colour" instead of "color", and "-ise" endings instead of "-ize" on words like "realise".

National Library of Australia Cataloguing-in-Publication entry:

Finlayson, Marina, author.
Moonborn / Marina Finlayson.
ISBN 9780994239136 (paperback)
A823.4

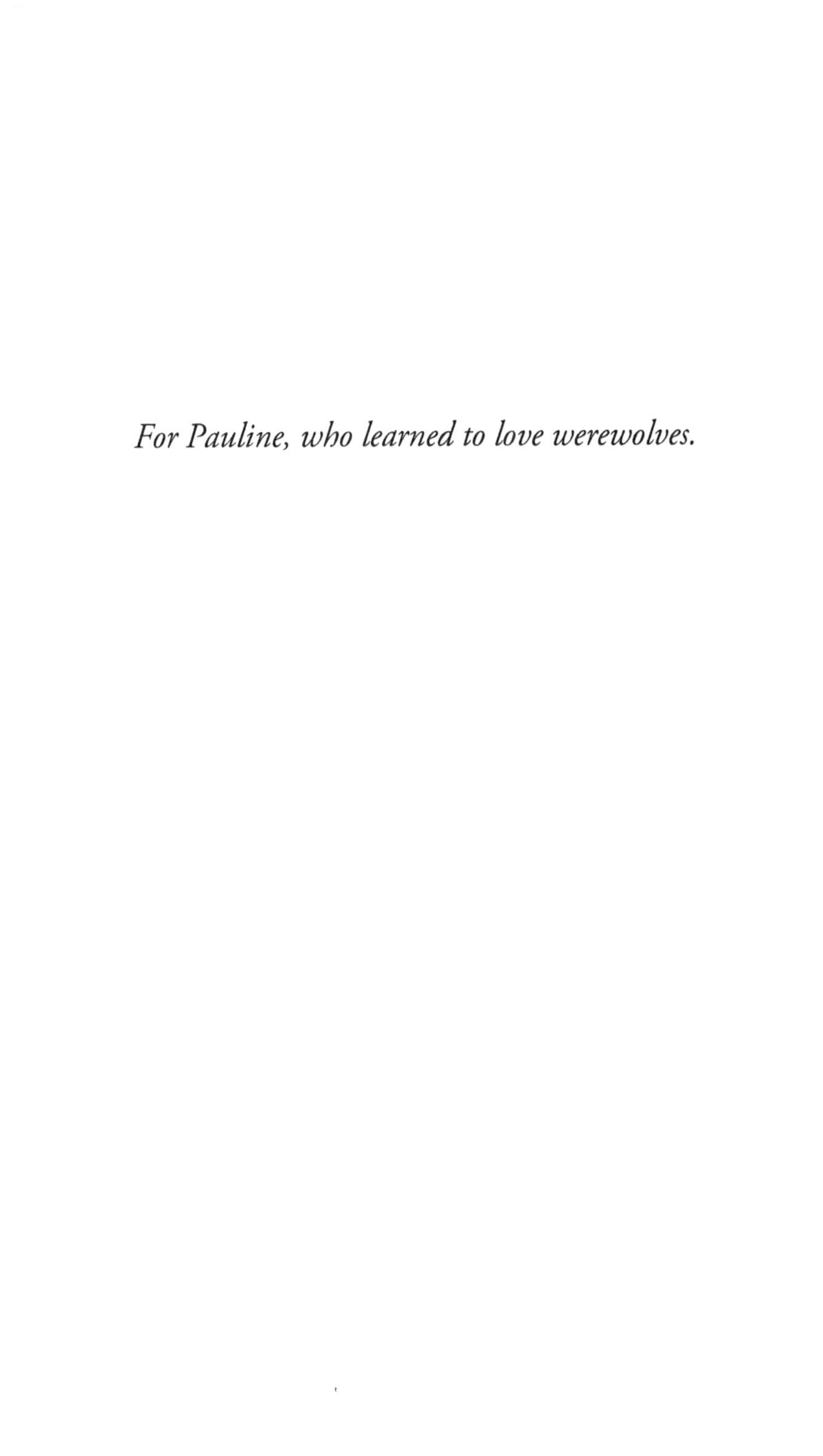

For Pauline, who learned to love werewolves.

FIRST MOON

Garth came out of his bedroom and sighed at the bodies sprawled all over the family room. Carly's auburn head was there, snuggled up close to that jerk Rhys Donohue. No sign of Rhys's father, Sean, but most of the younger pack members were there. You'd think they didn't have homes of their own, the way they parked themselves here every weekend. It was probably the lure of free beer and food, but it pissed Garth off. No privacy in his own home. He spent most weekends out somewhere else—anywhere else—to avoid seeing Rhys and his buddies twenty-four seven.

Garth shut his bedroom door, wishing it had a lock. He'd come home more than once to find pack members lounging on his bed as if they owned it. Nobody paid any attention to his protests, of course. He wasn't pack, so he had no status.

Carly stirred at the click of the door closing, and opened those fabulous blue eyes. She was the reason he stayed, the reason he put up with it all.

"Hey, Garth."

"Hey, Carly."

He headed for the kitchen. A quick breakfast and he was out of here. He shook some Coco Pops into a bowl and sat down at the big kitchen table.

Carly wandered in, wearing a T-shirt and knickers. She looked like an underwear model, with her long tanned legs and tousled just-got-out-of-bed hair. He tried not to look at her legs, and then of course all he could think of was her legs, and the way they disappeared under the T-shirt that just cleared her backside. Bloody shifters. None of them had the least idea of modesty. He supposed he should be grateful she'd even put the T-shirt on. He kept his eyes on his bowl.

"Did you sleep well?" she asked.

"Yeah. You?"

"We didn't really do a lot of sleeping."

He made the mistake of looking up as she answered, and caught the slow knowing smile. Immediately he felt the heat rush into his cheeks, and knew from the way her smile widened that she saw it.

Tossing her long red hair over her shoulder, she moved to block his way as he rose to take his empty bowl to the sink. The T-shirt had slipped, showing acres of bare skin. Hastily he looked away.

"You're so shy, Garth." She traced the line of his jaw, then tapped his bottom lip with her bright red nail. "I like that about you."

"I'm not shy. I just don't talk much." He sidestepped her and dumped the bowl, hating that her touch had started a fire in his belly. Just because she was five years older, she treated him like a kid, teasing him as if he were a teenager like Trevor. Or maybe it was because she was a shifter and he wasn't. She was the most gorgeous thing he'd ever seen. One day he'd like her to look at him and see a man.

But currently she only had eyes for Rhys, who now swaggered into the room, right on cue. Great. Garth could feel the milk in his stomach souring already. He should have skipped breakfast and gotten out of here before the rest of the pack roused.

Rhys eyed Garth's clothes—runners, shorts and T-shirt with logo—and smirked. "Heading to the gym again?"

"I work there."

"Bit of a waste of time, isn't it? You spend all your time there, and you're still a weakling."

"We can't all have werewolf muscles." He refused to get into a fight with Rhys this early in the morning. Especially not in front of Carly. Getting thrashed yet again wasn't going to do anything to raise her opinion of him. Nor would it impress his stepfather, the pack leader. Garth had lost count of the warnings Kevin had given him on letting his temper get the better of him.

Predictably, Rhys flexed his arms. Stupid git. Carly ran an approving hand over his bulging biceps.

"My, what big muscles you have." She fluttered her eyelashes at him, and he pulled her hard against him.

"All the better to grab you with, little girl."

Garth rolled his eyes and headed for the door, but Rhys stopped him with a hand on his arm. His grip was like steel.

"Maybe you should ask one of those pretty boys at the gym to give you some *personal* training." He sniggered. "You better not drop the soap in the shower, though."

Garth stared at him. When they were both younger he'd been on the receiving end of more than a few beatings from Rhys. That was why he'd started going to the gym in the first place. Should have known it would take more than a bit of weight-lifting to beat werewolf muscles. But for the last couple of years Rhys had confined himself to more subtle put-downs and dominance displays. Well, as subtle as someone like him could get. The guy was as dumb as rocks. "Let go."

Rhys stared back.

Wolves. They were all about the staring. Garth knew he should look away, let the jerk prove his dominance. Resistance only made it worse. Particularly when Carly was involved. But he'd never been very good at doing what he was supposed to.

Rhys's grip tightened.

"Let him go, babe," Carly said. "He's got to go to work."

"Yeah, some of us have real jobs," said Garth. Rhys supposedly worked as a bartender, but he seemed to have more nights off than on.

Rhys smirked. "You call adjusting some sweaty guy's jock strap a real job? Whatever turns you on, I guess."

That did it. Garth slammed his fist right into the middle of that smug grin. Felt Rhys's teeth cut his fingers, but he didn't care. Bastard had it coming.

"You little—" Rhys landed a punch of his own, though Garth was already moving, so it landed on his shoulder instead of his head. Garth felt a brief, vicious satisfaction as Rhys spat out blood and a broken tooth. Even though the werewolf bastard would be all healed up by lunchtime probably, and the tooth regrown.

"Stop it!" Carly shrieked.

Rhys's lips curled into a bloody snarl. He grabbed Garth by the shoulders and hurled him backwards onto the kitchen table. Garth landed with a crash, sending chairs flying, as Rhys followed with his fists. Garth rolled and twisted, but he couldn't evade all the blows. Rhys was so fast. Werewolf fast. It wasn't fair.

Garth lashed out with his foot and caught Rhys in the gut, halting the rain of blows long enough to scramble up and put the table between them. His ears rang, and one of his eyes was closing up already, but he didn't care. *Come and get it, you bastard.*

Rhys launched himself across the table, and they rolled across the floor, hands around each other's necks. Rhys had the better of him there, too, and Garth's vision began to spark with black dots.

"What the hell are you doing?"

He heard his brother's voice, and felt someone tugging at the hands around his neck, but he could barely see now. He bucked and tried to get a knee up to throw Rhys off, but there was no shifting him. The bastard had threatened to kill him a hundred times. Looked like today could be the day.

Suddenly the pressure on his throat was gone. Rhys's weight was gone. Garth jerked upright, heaving desperately for air. When the blackness cleared, he saw Kevin holding Rhys against the wall, the front of Rhys's shirt bunched up in Kevin's huge hand. Trevor stood to one side, watching Garth anxiously, but clearly not wishing to draw the alpha's attention.

"There a problem here, son?" Kevin drawled.

Rhys leaned his head away from the alpha. "No."

"Good. Cause I'd hate to have to tell my beta that his son was exiled from the pack for killing someone."

"I wasn't going to kill him."

Garth felt his throat. He could barely swallow. Sure felt like the bastard had been trying to kill him.

"We was just messing around." Rhys had obviously never learned to quit while he was ahead. "And he's not even a member of the pack. It's just Garth."

As if it was okay to kill someone who wasn't a pack member. Garth looked up at his stepfather, waiting for him to point this out, but all he said was: "Didn't look like messing around to me."

It's just Garth. He was twenty-two years old, a full-grown man, and the stepson of the pack's alpha. But he wasn't a wolf, so he was *just Garth*. Even his stepfather thought so. He clambered to his feet, fury welling in his heart.

"You can keep your messing around to yourself," said Kevin, "or you won't be welcome in my house. Understand?"

Rhys looked down at his feet sulkily. "Sure."

"Good." Kevin released Rhys with a little push. "You all right, Garth?"

"Fine." As if his stepfather gave a rat's arse.

Kevin stared at them all for a moment, and the three wolves in the room lowered their eyes before their leader. Garth made a point of staring back.

Kevin sighed. "Let's have no more trouble then. You got someplace else to be, Garth?"

"Just on my way to work."

Trevor drew in a sharp breath. "You're not going to go looking like that, are you?"

Garth looked down at himself. There was blood on his work shirt, and the left side of his jaw felt swollen. He was having trouble seeing out of his left eye. He probably looked like shit. Sure felt like it. But what else was he going to do? Stay here with a psycho werewolf who wanted him dead? Kevin hadn't even ordered Rhys out of the house.

Besides, he needed the money.

"I'll clean up when I get there."

Grimly he picked up his gym bag from the floor where he'd left it.

Carly leaned in and brushed her lips against his undamaged cheek. "Have a good day."

Just like a big sister. Probably trying to impress the alpha with how caring she was. Bit late now. She'd stood there and done nothing while her boyfriend belted into him. She smelled of cheap perfume and hot sex, with a side of alcohol. He wasn't too happy with her right now, but it still raised goosebumps on his skin when her long auburn hair trailed across his shoulder.

"Thanks." He stalked out without meeting anyone's eyes. Damn wolves. How could he hate them so much but still long to be one of them?

***

Garth parked under the jacarandas at the back of the carpark. Management didn't like the staff taking all the best parking spots near the door. Gym bag over his shoulder, he strode across the carpark, still fuming, his swollen face throbbing in time with his footsteps. He'd caught a glimpse in the rear vision mirror of his bloodshot eye, half-buried in puffy skin that was already shiny and blue. Not a pretty sight.

Inside, the receptionist did a double-take.

"What happened to you?"

"Fell down the stairs." He kept walking, leaving her squawking in his wake.

In the locker room, he saw that the damage was as bad as he'd thought. But he wasn't going home. Home. Huh. That was a joke. He felt more at home here, surrounded by people paying for his time. At least they appreciated him, even looked up to him. At "home" he was nothing. Less than nothing.

The shift manager took one look at his face and told him to take the day off.

"I'm fine," Garth insisted.

"Fine? You look like you've been in a brawl. Not exactly the image we want to project to our clients."

No way was he leaving. He needed to work off some of the anger threatening to burst free. "Nobody gives a shit what I look like. All they care about is my results. I'm the most requested PT on staff."

That was pretty hard to argue with. The shift manager knew it as well as he did. "Don't swear."

Garth checked his appointments. "And I have a new client this morning. She's been waiting weeks. You going to tell her I can't make the appointment because I'm not pretty enough today?"

"Fine. But you feel any dizziness, have any vision problems, you get yourself to the doctor. You collapse on the job, I don't want any workers' comp claims, you understand?"

"Whatever."

He met his first client, a young guy trying to bulk up for a bodybuilding competition, and worked alongside him until they were both shiny with sweat, and Garth's muscles knew they existed. He tried to clear his mind and focus on what his body was doing, but that natural flow state eluded him today. All he could think of was the smirk on Rhys's face, the pity in Carly's eyes.

"Thanks, man," the guy said at the end of the hour. "That was a tough session. You're like a machine!"

If only he was a machine. A robot like C-3PO maybe, only not so prissy. R2-D2 had more balls. Someone who didn't have to deal with all these stupid feelings. He was such a boiling mess of impotent rage, shame, and longing, he hardly knew which way was up. Couldn't think straight, couldn't see straight.

For a moment he thought Carly had come—to check on him, maybe even apologise. A redheaded girl approached, long legs in tight bike shorts. But it wasn't Carly, of course. He'd never seen this girl before, though she smiled as if she knew him.

"Hi, Garth?" She held out her hand. "I'm Deb, your ten o'clock appointment."

"Oh, hi." The new client. "Come and we'll get all your details."

He wiped his face on his towel, wincing a little.

"Are you sure this is a good time?" Her brown eyes were shadowed with concern. "What happened to you? Are you feeling okay?"

"Sure, I'm fine." His head throbbed like a heavy metal track. Nothing a few painkillers wouldn't fix. "Slipped on the stairs this morning. Landed on my face."

She winced in sympathy. "Ouch. Sounds painful. Are you sure you don't want to reschedule? That eye looks pretty bad."

She followed him toward the interview room.

"I've had worse."

"Really? Do you fall down a lot?"

Idiot. He'd forgotten who he was talking to for a moment. She reminded him so much of Carly.

"Yeah, I can be pretty clumsy." He shut the door and waved her to a seat. "But let's talk about you for a while. You say you'd like some help with your training. What are your goals?"

"I'd like to build some muscle, mainly. I'm pretty happy with my weight." She laughed, a bright tinkling sound. "As much as any woman ever is, I guess. But I need to work on my strength. I don't want to look like Arnold Schwarzenegger, obviously, but a bit more definition than I've got would be good.

"Right." He wrote *muscle definition* on her sheet. Seemed like everyone wanted bigger muscles these days. Including him. If you added up all the hours he'd spent in the gym it would probably be months, but the best way to build muscle still seemed to be getting a werewolf to bite you. No workout regime, however stringent, could top those shifter muscles. He'd come closer today against Rhys, but he knew perfectly well that if Kevin hadn't hauled Rhys off when he had, he could easily be dead.

He started taking Deb's measurements, so they'd have a baseline to compare progress with, whipping the tape measure around her biceps with professional detachment. She smiled up at him, admiration in her big brown eyes. That only made him angrier. It wasn't *this* woman that he wanted.

Oh, sure, to *her* his body would look pretty good. All those hours of work had paid off in a way that would have made any other man happy. But he'd seen real strength, and it didn't come with bodybuilding. There was no way he'd ever be able to take that bastard Rhys down. No way Carly would ever look at him the way Deb was looking at him now.

He measured her calves, did the usual hip and waist measurements, then ran some tests on her flexibility. All the while, his mind wandered elsewhere, worrying at the problem like a dog with a bone. Surrounded by wolves, this dog was never going to get the bone. He would always be the mongrel everyone kicked away. Why did he stay? Why not just move away and leave the pack? It wasn't as if they'd ever made him feel welcome. What would he miss by going?

Carly's face came to him again. God, he was a fool. She barely knew he existed, treated him like a little brother or, worse still, a joke. And wherever she went, Rhys went, too. He had no chance as long as Rhys could push him around like a little kid.

"Okay!" He forced a smile, though it made his face hurt even worse. Probably didn't look too appealing either, but Deb didn't seem to mind. "Enough paperwork. Let's get out there and see what you can do."

He put her on the first machine, watching her technique with a critical eye. "Keep your back straighter." He adjusted her posture, and she leaned into his hand.

Other girls liked him just fine. He never had any shortage of dates, and there were always girls at the gym making eyes at him. But the one girl he wanted had no interest.

He shoved his hands in his pockets, forcing himself to relax his clenched fists. Seemed like he was always angry these days. Either angry or miserable. He was sick of living like this. Something had to change.

Maybe that something was him.

He'd thought about it before, of course. As a child he'd begged his mother for the Change like other kids begged for bikes. But she'd always refused him. Reminded him how many people didn't survive the Change. Said he didn't understand what it would mean if he did.

Well, that was a load of bollocks. He'd grown up in the middle of the goddamn pack. He was probably the most qualified non-werewolf alive to know the changes becoming a werewolf would bring to his body and his life. As a child, there'd been nothing he'd wanted more. Lately he was starting to feel that way again.

It wouldn't be easy, though. His mother and her alpha husband wouldn't allow him to "risk his life for nothing", as his mother put it, so there was no use asking. He'd have to find some other way to get what he wanted.

He watched Deb as he put her through her paces, doing his job efficiently, but in his mind he was seeing another girl, with that same long red hair. Seeing the admiration in her eyes as he joined the pack stronger, fitter, faster. He'd show her he wasn't just someone to be looked down on and pitied. He'd make her see him as he truly was: a man worthy of being her mate.

And that bastard Rhys would get what was coming to him.

***

Trevor hoisted the backpack containing the heavy length of chain and the first-aid kit onto his back as if it were empty, and Garth felt the familiar stab of envy at his baby brother's strength.

"Wish this was silver," Trevor said.

"What the hell for?" Garth locked the car and headed off down the trail. Long fingers of shadow stretched ahead of him on the rough earth. Only an hour or so until sunset. They needed to move if they wanted to be well away from civilisation before the moon rose. "I'm not bringing that shit anywhere near you. One scratch and you're dead."

"I'm just worried." Garth cast a glance back at his brother. Trevor's young face showed a strange mix of emotions: nerves at what they were attempting warred with the thrill of his first time out under the full moon. "I don't want to hurt you."

"Can't make an omelette without breaking some eggs."

Trevor pushed up beside him and gestured impatiently. "I mean really hurt you. What if—what if I can't stop?"

"That's what the chain's for, genius. Relax, would you?"

Trevor took a deep breath, scenting the air. Garth couldn't smell anything except the faint tang of eucalyptus. Plenty of gums crowded the track, with scrubby low undergrowth filling the gaps between. The way meandered around big outcroppings of sandstone, following the rise and fall of the land. There were a hundred such trails in this stretch of bushland, but at this time on a winter's afternoon they had this one to themselves. Just as well. Garth had purposely chosen a remote part of the national park for the evening's adventure.

Trevor strode out, his skinny teenage frame belying the shifter strength that lurked within. "Dad's gonna freak when he finds out."

"Kevin's always freaking about something. He'll get over it."

Trevor cast him a sideways glance. "You know, it wouldn't kill you to call him Dad sometimes. He's asked you often enough."

"He's not—"

"—your dad, I know, I know. I'm just saying. You guys might get along better if you tried to meet him halfway once in a while."

Trevor forged ahead, leaving Garth to glare at his back. Bloody kid. What did he know? Son of the pack leader and his mate, his life ticked all the boxes. Favoured status in the pack: tick. Shifter strength and power: tick. He had no idea what it was like to be the outsider, tolerated but not really included. Garth was just the leftover from their mother's previous marriage, before she became a wolf herself, that weak human kid who'd grown up underfoot, but never been part of the pack family.

"At least we managed to give Rhys the slip, huh?" Trevor threw a fierce grin over his shoulder. Garth couldn't help grinning back; the kid's excitement was infectious. At seventeen, he was considered too young to run with the pack at full moon, so every month he'd spent the night locked in the reinforced basement at the pack house. This would be his first time running free. If he was lucky he might catch a fox or a rabbit. Maybe even an unwary possum or koala out of its tree. There were bigger animals, too, in the national parks: kangaroos, and introduced species such as wild pigs and even some deer, but a lone wolf would struggle to bring one down. Particularly a juvenile wolf on his first real hunt.

"Bet he'll cop some stick for that." The thought gave Garth a warm glow of happiness. Karma was a bitch. Rhys Donohue could catch on fire and Garth wouldn't bother pissing on him. The guy was a worm who thought he was hot shit because his daddy was the pack's beta. Most of Garth's worst childhood memories involved Rhys Donohue's smug grin in the background of some humiliation or other.

"Couldn't happen to a nicer guy." At seventeen to Rhys's twenty-eight, even the pack leader's favoured son came in for some heat from Rhys. A pack was a strict hierarchy, and there wasn't much lower in the pecking order than a juvenile wolf. Only the babies and seven-year-old McKenna had less status. And Garth, of course.

But all that was going to change. Soon Trevor would be eighteen and considered a full adult member of the pack, old enough to join the endless jockeying for status. And Garth …

After tonight Garth would no longer be the outsider, pitied and barely tolerated. Carly's eyes wouldn't slide right over him whenever a wolf was in the room. No more drunken affection, as if he were a little kid or a favoured pet. She'd see him as a real man. A better bloody one than that jerk Donohue.

As the shadows lengthened, they continued past the fork in the track and took the winding trail that climbed deeper into the wilderness. Garth had been this way many times before and knew that, further on, the trail opened into a natural clearing in the bush, surrounded by tall straight gums and a couple of pine trees that had been seeded in amongst the natives by birds. Also tall and straight but much easier to climb for a man in a hurry.

Only the top of the sun's disk still showed above the trees. Garth eyed the fiery orb and picked up the pace a little.

"How are we doing for time?"

"Soon," said Trevor. His eyes caught the glow of the setting sun. They were still blue; no sign yet of the wolf's yellow surfacing, but it wouldn't be long. The full moon would rise in the east only moments after the sun set. Garth cast an anxious glance over his shoulder, but the eastern horizon was still clear.

In another couple of minutes the trail opened out into the clearing, and some of his tension eased, though a knot of nerves still lodged in his gut. The path continued into the trees on the far side, disappearing around a rock and up the hill out of sight, but this was their destination. Trevor shrugged off the heavy pack and stretched with pleasure, turning his face up to the deepening blue of the sky.

Garth upended the backpack, spilling the thick chain onto the grass with a clink and clatter of metal.

"Over here." He gestured his brother to the base of a large pine whose sturdy branches began just above ground level and continued in regular steps all the way up the thick trunk. It would be easy as climbing a ladder. He took the first-aid kit up a safe distance and lashed it to a branch. Beside it he secured a heavy-duty torch. Trevor watched his preparations, shifting uneasily from foot to foot at the base of the tree.

"Did you bring the straps to tie yourself on? I don't want you falling out of the tree in the middle of the night because you've fallen asleep."

Garth glanced down through the pine needles at the anxious face upturned to him. "Will you quit worrying and get your gear off? You sound like Mum."

"I just don't want anything to happen to you."

He jumped down and placed his hands firmly on his younger brother's shoulders. It looked like the kid was never going to match him for height, but he was a great guy.

"The only thing that's going to happen to me is I'll finally get what I've wanted all my life." He felt again Carly's lips on his cheek. But this wasn't about her. Or not just about her, at least. He was sick of being the outsider looking in. He was somebody, and there was only one way to prove that in this family.

Trevor's mouth twisted in a wry smile, but he obediently pulled off his jeans and shirt, leaving them in a neat pile with his boots at the foot of the tree. "That's not all you'll get. You're also going to land in a shitload of trouble with Dad when he finds out. We both are. Are you really sure about this?"

Garth picked up the chain and started winding its length around his brother's body. Trevor stood patiently through this procedure. "Absolutely. Trouble's my middle name."

Garth gave a final tug and secured the end. It wasn't meant to hold Trevor all night, just long enough to give Garth a headstart up that tree.

"Tight enough?"

"It's fine."

But Trevor wasn't looking at him as he spoke; his gaze was turned to the east. In the deepening twilight his eyes suddenly shone a golden yellow. Garth drew in a sharp breath. He'd never been so close to someone during the change before, and his heartbeat picked up speed.

He followed his brother's unfocused gaze to the east and saw a round sliver of moon peek above the treetops. Trevor collapsed in a jangle of chains. A strange noise, half groan, half growl, burst from his lips.

Garth took a step back from the writhing body at his feet. This was the part that always grossed him out. The crunching of breaking bone made him want to heave. Trevor whimpered and moaned as his skeleton rearranged itself, thrashing against the chains like a soul in torment. Did it feel as bad as it sounded? If all went well he'd find out for himself soon enough.

Coarse dark hair sprouted all over Trevor's naked body, growing so fast Garth could hear the faint hiss of it. His brother was unrecognisable now, his face distorting as his jaw cracked and lengthened and those mad yellow eyes shifted in his skull. The thrashing body had four legs now, long and lean, each ending in a wolf's padded foot. One of those legs had slipped free of the restricting chains already. Garth swallowed hard and edged a little closer to the safety of the tree.

The plan had seemed a lot better in the daylight than it did now, with a werewolf writhing at his feet and the darkness closing in on him.

Are you a man or not? This is what you want!

He took a firm step closer as thick, dark fur rippled in a final wave across the wolf's face. Now or never. The beast lay still, watching him with a mad gleam in its amber eyes. No sign of his brother's humanity remained. It was always like this on full moon night. Any other night a wolf could choose whether or not to change shape, and still keep some part of his human purpose and control intact. But the full moon was like a powerful drug that sang through the wolf's veins, irresistible as the tide. At full moon there were no choices, no decisions, just animal bloodlust and pure instinct. Unfortunately it was also the only time when a werewolf's bite could create a new werewolf. Which explained why most wolves were born, not turned. A werewolf under the influence of the full moon rarely stopped at one bite.

The wolf growled, a low rumbling that crept up Garth's spine and lifted all the little hairs on the back of his neck. No use telling himself this was only Trevor, though he knew Trevor's wolf form almost as well as his human one. This was emphatically *not* Trevor, not now, not tonight. Given half a chance he'd rip Garth's throat out and guzzle his life's blood without the slightest hesitation.

Nevertheless … Time to do what he'd come to do, before he lost his nerve completely. He held his left arm out to the bound wolf. Its lip quivered in a snarl, its mad eyes locked on his. Then it convulsed and hurled itself on him, chains and all.

He went down with its teeth sinking deep into his arm, tearing at his flesh. Hot agony shot through him. With a shout of terror he fought it off, the chains ice-cold on his flesh where it lay on top of him. Its claws tore at him, vicious jaws snapping in his face. He rolled, throwing its snarling weight off him, and scrambled free.

Bucking and twisting like a mad thing, the wolf fought its way clear of the chains. Garth lunged for the pine. Its rough bark scraped his hands, and pine-scented branches whacked him in the face as he heaved himself up. Below, the wolf snarled. Garth looked down as it hurled itself after him.

The chain, still tangled around one leg, brought it up short, but it sank its teeth into one booted foot. The thing jumped like it had springs in its bloody legs. As its claws scrabbled for purchase on the trunk, Garth dangled precariously from one hand and kicked it hard in the face with his free foot. It slammed back to the ground. Thank God for upper body strength. All those hours of chin-ups had paid off.

"Christ on a friggin pogo stick." Garth wasted no time pulling himself higher, not stopping till he'd gained the branch where the first-aid kit awaited him. That had been way too close. He sat, one arm wrapped around the trunk for a moment, waiting for his panicked breathing to return to something approaching normal. Every muscle trembled with exertion and fear. *Way* too close. How high could the damn thing jump, for God's sake? It wasn't a bloody kangaroo.

He cradled his injured arm against his chest and peered down through the branches. The wolf paced back and forth at the base of the tree, its vicious face turned up to his, mad yellow eyes catching the light of the rising moon. The chain clanked along behind it, snagging on rocks and small bushes. It was still tangled round the wolf's body and one back leg. Looked like his brother wouldn't be doing any hunting tonight after all.

He examined the bite in the light of the torch. The deep puncture marks hurt like hell and a small chunk of flesh had been ripped away, leaving an ugly wound that bled freely. He bound it as well as he could one-handed, then tried to get comfortable in the hard fork of the tree. The damn wolf never took its eyes off him the whole time.

It was going to be a long night.

***

Towards dawn the ache from his arm had spread through his whole body. He'd got up every hour and moved around in the tree, to keep from getting too stiff and to keep himself awake. Climbing one-handed was tricky though, and getting trickier with every passing hour. He knew the fever had kicked in when he started to sweat. It was the middle of winter, for God's sake. No one stuck up a pine tree out in the cold should be sweating. It was then he'd used the straps to secure himself to the tree. After putting up with a night like this he wasn't going to end it by sliding into unconsciousness and becoming wolf takeaway.

So he sat on his branch, shivering and sweating like the world's ugliest bird, and watched the wolf. It still lay at the bottom of his tree, quiet again, though now and then it would writhe and snap at the entangling chain. The single-minded focus of its gaze unnerved him.

"Sorry about the chain," he said.

One pointed ear flicked at the sound of his voice, but it gave no sign that it understood what he was saying.

"If I'd done a better job you could have been off hunting instead of hanging around." Of course the wolf might also have caught him before he made it to safety, so he wasn't all *that* sorry. A shame his brother's big chance to run free under the moon hadn't worked out, especially since he'd be locked up and watched even more carefully now until he was officially old enough to join with the pack, but oh well. Trevor would just have to be patient. He'd be eighteen in a few months, old enough to be accepted as a full member.

Garth's arm throbbed in time with his heartbeat; the whole left side of his body felt like it was on fire. He wiped sweat out of his eyes and peered at his watch. The illuminated numbers said 6:03. Only another hour, then, until the sun rose and he could get out of this goddamn tree. Halle-bloody-lujah.

He peered down at the wolf, which gazed back unblinking. If Trevor weren't so young, he might have been back in human shape already. The older wolves regained control faster after the initial bloodrush of the moon. Shame. Garth shifted uncomfortably against the straps. As it was, Trevor might have to climb up here and help him down. With each passing moment Garth felt himself weakening, losing himself to a tide of heat and sickness. His vision danced and blurred. He even thought he saw another wolf peering between the trees on the far side of the clearing.

No, wait.

The wolf at the base of the tree rose suddenly to its feet with a clank of chains, a warning growl rumbling deep in its chest. It turned to face the intruder. There *was* another wolf. It slipped into the moonlit clearing, followed by another. And then another.

Garth blinked, trying to clear his blurred vision, then groaned. He knew those three. The first wolf had a distinctive white ruff around its neck. What was that arsehole Rhys doing here? And of course the other two were Jensen and Benedetti, tagging along as usual like two balls bouncing after a dick. How had they found them?

The three stalked across the clearing, fanning out so that Trevor couldn't rush all three at once. Hackles up, teeth bared, their intention was plain. And Trevor was hampered by the damn chain. Even without it, he had no chance three against one.

"Hey!" Garth's voice came out raw and croaky. The advancing wolves ignored him, their attention riveted by the lone wolf backed against the tree. "What are you doing, you jerks?"

He wrenched an ancient pine cone off the nearest branch and hurled it at Rhys's ugly head, but his aim was off, and it clattered harmlessly against the trees on the far side of the small clearing. The effort caused such a wave of pain he nearly passed out. His left arm had swollen to twice its normal size, and throbbed with an agony that seemed all out of proportion to the severity of the wound.

The three wolves paced closer, their growling an ominous music that filled the little clearing. What the hell were they doing?

"Get away from him," Garth shouted. "Kevin'll kill you if you hurt him."

Did they even understand him? With the moon still squatting atop the western horizon, it seemed unlikely. Stupid bloody animals. What had brought them here, when the pack was supposed to be running in the Blue Mountains?

A twig snapped in the darkness under the trees. A man appeared, a familiar lanky shape clad in a flannelette shirt with the sleeves rolled up despite the winter cold.

"Donohue!" Garth wouldn't normally welcome the sight of the pack's beta, but for once his hated authority could do some good. It was no surprise to see him in human form at this time on a full moon night. After Kevin himself he was the oldest member of the pack; he'd probably been human for a couple of hours. "Get your son and his idiot friends under control, before they do something stupid."

"You trying to tell me what to do again, Garth?" The older man's tone was mild, but Garth's good fist clenched reflexively. Something about Sean Donohue's face just made him want to punch it. "What are you boys doing out here? Trevor's supposed to be locked up safe at home with the other juvies."

Sean walked closer, his feet crunching on grass now touched with frost, until he stood between his son and Jensen. The wolves ignored him: they could smell he was one of their own, and he laid his hand on the white fur of Rhys's neck. That didn't stop the big wolf growling—if anything his deep rumbling growl increased in volume.

"Whatcha doing up that tree, boy? Is that your blood I smell?" Donohue had a look of concern on his smarmy face so fake it was all Garth could do not to lob another pine cone right into it. "Hope you haven't gone and done something stupid. Your father's not going to be happy."

Garth gritted his teeth. *My father's dead.* "Why don't you take Trevor home with you then, if you're so worried, and I'll come down."

Donohue shook his head. "I'm surprised at you, Garth, really I am. Smart boy like you—you've been around the pack long enough to know how this works." He stepped back, out of the circle of wolves. At his signal the three leapt forward, snarling. The darkness at the foot of the tree came alive with snarls and yelps.

"Call them off!" Garth strained to see what was happening in the shadows. His brother seemed to be buried alive under a writhing, snapping mass of wolves. Trevor burst free with a high scream of pain, but the chain restricted his movement, and Rhys leapt for his throat again.

"He needs to learn obedience." Rhys's father had to raise his voice to be heard over the noise of battle.

"But they're killing him!" Frantically Garth looked for a weapon. There was a small pair of scissors in the first-aid kit, meant for cutting bandages. What good would that be against three full-grown wolves? But it was all he had. He couldn't just sit here and watch them tear his brother to shreds. With shaking fingers he unclipped the strap that held him in place, but when he tried to climb down to the next branch his feet slipped out from under him and he fell instead.

One of the wolves looked up as he snagged a branch and halted his rough descent, hunger on its snarling face. If he went down there he was dead. The dark clearing swam before his eyes and the world reeled around his tree while he clung to the trunk, fighting to stay conscious.

When the noises below stopped, Garth opened his eyes to see the last of the wolves disappearing into the bush. His brother lay unmoving at the base of the tree. Sean Donohue stood in the centre of the clearing, watching them both, brawny arms folded. The sky to the east was flooded with pink light.

"Rise and shine, boy. It's a brand new day." Clouds of steam huffed out with each word in the chilly air.

"Kevin's going to kill you when he finds out what you've done."

The beta laughed. "You really don't get it, do you? Kevin sent me. There are rules, boy. You step out of line, you pay the price. You remind your brother of that when he wakes up."

He gave Garth a mocking wave and turned to follow the wolves.

For long moment Garth clung there, watching his brother, willing him to move, to wake up. Something. He could still see the moon's disk through a gap in the trees, half-sunk below the horizon. If the three wolves came back … Too bad. He couldn't wait any longer.

He reached for the first-aid kit, but his groping fingers had lost their dexterity, and all he managed to do was knock it into the darkness below. Well, that was one way of getting it down. Slowly, painfully, he began easing himself down the tree after it, his whole body crying out at the rough treatment it had received. Though dawn's light filled the clearing, he could barely see what he was doing; his vision was speckled with darkness and fevered red dots and squiggles. He fell from the lower branches, the breath slamming out of him as he hit the ground. For a long moment he lay there, stunned, while blackness prickled in his vision. Then he forced himself up. Trevor needed him.

He staggered to his brother's side. Trevor was human again, covered in ugly slashes and bites, but his pulse was strong. Shifters had supernatural healing powers. Just as well, considering the amount of blood staining the ground around his brother's body. Although maybe not all of it was his. Hopefully Trevor had managed to inflict a few wounds of his own on those arseholes. Garth rolled him over. Geez, what a mess.

Trevor's eyelids fluttered as the first rays of the rising sun hit his face and he groaned. Beneath his sickness and pain Garth felt hot rage course through him. Those bastards! How dared they do this to his brother?

"Easy there, mate." He scrabbled around in the pine needles that blanketed the ground until he found the first-aid kit. Then he ripped a gauze pad from its packaging and pressed it to the biggest slash on his brother's neck, which had come dangerously close to an artery. It still leaked blood sluggishly. Trevor moaned and his hand twitched towards Garth's.

His eyes, when they opened, were clear blue again, no sign now of the wolf's madness.

Garth leaned forward anxiously. "How do you feel?"

"Like shit. How about you?"

"Same."

"Great." He pushed Garth's hand away and held the gauze in place himself, then struggled upright and propped himself against the tree trunk. His face was pale and drawn with pain. "It's a long walk back to the car."

"I know." Garth sighed and fumbled the phone out of his back pocket. Not the way he would have liked to do it, but beggars couldn't be choosers. Neither of them was fit to hike back to the car park. He dialled Mum's number. "Houston, we have a problem."

SECOND MOON

He didn't remember much of the month that followed. If he wasn't feverish, he was unconscious, and when he wasn't unconscious he felt so bloody awful that he just lay in his bed staring at the ceiling, too miserable even to be tired of that unchanging view. Now and then a pack member would poke their head round the door as if to check he was still alive, but for the most part Mum kept everyone away.

And if there was one thing guaranteed to make a bloke feel like a naughty child again, it was having your mother fussing around your sick bed like you were still three years old.

"How's Trevor?" he asked, the first moment he could string two thoughts together. That was nearly two weeks into his illness.

"Fine," was all she said, but the way her mouth pursed, as if she were sucking lemons, spoke volumes. About her distaste for violence, the stupidities of young men, and particularly her disappointment in him for leading his brother into harm's way. "Which is more than can be said for you."

"I'm feeling much better," he lied.

"What were you thinking, Garth?" She laid down the spoon she'd been using to feed him soup and stared at him in frustration. "Why would you take such a risk?"

Garth rolled his head on the pillow, turning away from her glare. "How was I to know those bastards were following us?"

"Not that. Why did you let him bite you?"

Surprised that for once her concern was for him, he turned back to look at her. She picked up the spoon and thrust another mouthful of soup at him. "Why would anyone *choose* this life? If you even survive the Change. Because there's no guarantee of that, you know."

"I know." Statistically, if a victim survived the initial attack, there was still only a fifty-fifty chance of making a successful transformation at the next full moon. But he was young and strong; his chances were much better than that. Mum knew that, too. Anyway, what was her beef? Life as the pack's alpha female seemed to suit her just fine. He shrugged. "Seemed like a good idea at the time."

"Oh, don't be flippant, Garth. This is serious. I've never met such a pig-headed little … Have you even thought about what being a wolf means?" She gave him a disgusted look. "No, of course you haven't. How are *you* going to fit into a pack? Even as a child you couldn't stand being told what to do. You're the most independent person I know."

He stared back at her. As the newest member of the pack—if he made it that far—he'd be at the bottom of the pecking order. *Rhys can push me around and no one will blink.* And of course the jerk would take every opportunity to rub his nose in it. The soup sat like lead in the bottom of his stomach.

Well, he'd just have to fight his way to the top of the heap, then, wouldn't he? Put the little shit in his place.

"You didn't even think of that, did you? I can tell from your face. So what *were* you thinking?"

He shifted restlessly. "Why does it matter? It's done now."

She made a noise of exasperation and stood, taking the tray with her. "Yes, it's done. And you'll have to live with the consequences for the rest of your life."

One of those consequences made itself known a few minutes later. Kevin came in and shut the door firmly.

"Your mother said you were awake."

"Uh-huh."

Kevin glared at him from under thick, shaggy brows. He had grey-blue eyes, very similar to Garth's own, ironically enough. People who didn't realise he was Garth's stepfather often commented on the "likeness". Those eyes could change colour with Kevin's moods, and now reflected the iron-cold grey of a winter sea.

"You know your mother's going to be devastated if you don't make it through the Change. I can't believe you could put her through this."

"I'll be fine. She made it through all right."

"She had no choice—she was attacked. You did this deliberately. You manipulated your brother into helping you. How's he going to feel if you die? Did you stop to think about that?"

"I'm young. I'm strong."

"I've seen people who were young and strong before, who didn't make it through. That's just like you, so sure of yourself when you know nothing about it."

"So you don't actually care if I die, only that it will upset Mum and Trevor?"

"Don't put words into my mouth, Garth. I didn't think you cared what I thought."

"I don't."

Kevin laughed, a short, bitter sound. "Then you're an even bigger fool than I suspected." His eyes met Garth's, and now there was a tinge of yellow in the grey, a hint of wolf. "Because if you live I will be your alpha, and you have no idea yet what that means." He held up a hand as Garth opened his mouth. "Oh, you think you do, but you don't. No idea at all. You are going to care what I think more than you ever dreamed possible. You'll care so much you'll probably regret coming up with this stupid scheme in the first place. And there'll be nothing you can do about it. There's no backing out now. Once a wolf, always a wolf."

"I can live with that." Garth tipped his chin up defiantly. It was hard to look imposing when you were stretched out in bed in a pair of sweaty pyjamas.

"I sure hope so. Because that is the first and last time you do something so selfish. Pack comes first, and you don't do anything without my say-so."

Garth shrugged, and looked past his stepfather's ear as if he weren't that interested in the conversation. That always got Kevin's back up.

Predictably, Kevin stiffened. For a long moment the only sound in the room was their breathing.

"Well," Kevin said at last, "I can see there's no point talking to you now. Things will be different after full moon. You've chosen a hard path for yourself, but there's no choice now but to walk it, or you'll end up a wolf without a pack. And I wouldn't wish that on my worst enemy."

***

Long days passed, blending into one another. Garth still felt like a limp rag, slipping in and out of fevered dreams, till all of a sudden one day he didn't. He woke with the dawn, and he just knew. Today was the day. The promise of the moon sent a shiver of energy through him. He bounded out of bed like a kid on Christmas morning, then nearly fell as a wave of dizziness caught him. The sound of him staggering brought his mother, with Trevor hard on her heels.

"How are you feeling?"

No matter how many times he answered her question, she never seemed satisfied with the answer.

"Better. Much better." Although weak as a newborn pup. And ravenous.

"Tonight's full moon."

He nodded. "I can tell."

His skin crawled with an itchy, tingly sense of anticipation, as if a thousand ants marched back and forth across his body.

"The whole pack's going to be there tonight for you," Trevor said, shifting from foot to foot as if he, too, felt the moon's pull, fizzing with restless energy. "Even the babies are coming."

Garth nodded. The last time the pack had awaited the judgment of the moon would have been after his mother was bitten, way back before Trevor was even born. Everyone would gather to watch the potential new wolf's first transformation. If successful, the new pack member would then be welcomed by and bond with the other members. If not …

No need to think about that. He wasn't planning on dying tonight.

Well before sunset, the pack was on the move. A convoy of four-wheel drives took an old dirt trail deep into the vast bushland of the Blue Mountains National Park, jouncing over the grooves in the rough trail. Kevin drove the way he did everything, with a calm assumption of his own competence, big hairy hands holding the wheel in a firm but not tight grip. Garth sat in the back with Trevor and watched the clouds of dust billowing up from the convoy's wheels and tried to imagine what his first change would feel like.

Some people said it was like childbirth: it got easier every time. Others said no, it was like childbirth because being a wolf was so damn good you forgot how painful getting there was until you were in the middle of it again. Maybe he'd be one of the lucky ones who shrugged the whole thing off. He was no stranger to pain, but he'd be just as happy to get through it without passing out from the agony, or puking up his guts like some juvenile wolves did, thanks very much.

In the rear vision mirror he caught his stepfather watching him, but Kevin said nothing. They hadn't spoken since that day in his room, when Kevin had basically said "it's my way or the highway". It had pissed him off at the time, but it hardly seemed important now, with the coming of the moon singing in his blood. It was all he could think of, and when the cars at last rolled to a stop and they all got out to continue on foot, he turned instinctively to face the east, where the moon would soon rise.

"Let's move, people," Kevin said, and they did, with very little noise or fuss. Janice carried Margie, who was only two, while her older daughter Mac skipped ahead, very excited at seven to be joining the grown-ups for the full moon for the first time. The twins were barely six months old, and their parents carried one each. Normally they would have taken turns to stay at the pack house with the little ones and Trevor, all locked safely away while the pack hunted, but for an occasion like tonight, every member of the pack needed to be there.

Carly walked a little ahead with Rhys, and sometimes Garth caught a glimpse past the bodies in front of him of her long auburn hair swinging. The pack travelled roughly in order of seniority, except that his mother walked at the back with him, instead of taking her usual place at Kevin's side at the head of the line.

The winter air had a distinct bite to it, but exercise soon warmed him. The pack moved fast down the trail, even burdened with the little ones, and Kevin soon led them off the track and into the grey-green bush. How could he tell where he was going? The scrubby undergrowth and the straight pale trunks of the gums all looked the same to Garth's eyes.

Even Garth, fit as he was, began to breathe deeply as the ground climbed upwards. They jumped a small stream then emerged from the trees onto a windswept hill. Still they climbed, the sun a fiery sinking orb in their faces, till they reached the top. Huge boulders, smoothed by centuries of weather, lay exposed to the elements as if scattered from a giant's hand. Behind one loomed the entrance to a cave, which little Mac rushed to explore with a cry of pleasure. The rest of the pack gathered in a loose circle in a sheltered spot among the boulders.

"It's nearly time." His mother looked to the west, where the sun had disappeared below the trees. "How do you feel?"

"Strange," he admitted. The moon hadn't risen in the east yet, but it could only be moments away. His blood sang with anticipation, and tremors of heat flushed through him.

"Better get your gear off, boy," Sean Donohue said. The beta was bare-chested, and had kicked off his shoes. "Don't want to rip your clothes and have nothing to go home in, do you?"

His son appeared at his side, already naked. Rhys had enough hair just on his chest to coat most of a full-grown wolf.

"I hear the pain's worse if you're not born to it." He smirked at Garth. "Hope you can take it."

That was one pack member who wouldn't shed any tears if Garth proved to be one of the people that didn't live through their first change.

"Be quiet, Rhys," Garth's mother snapped.

She was already disrobing, folding each item of clothing neatly as she removed it. Garth felt his face flush as he took off his own T-shirt under Rhys's mocking eye. Bloody wolves. They were such a pack of exhibitionists. This was going to take some getting used to. He tried not to look at anyone else as he followed her example.

When he looked up, Kevin stood in front of him, still clothed. In his hands he held a knife in a leather sheath. Garth had never seen it before.

"You're not changing?" Everyone else was naked, awaiting the moon.

"Some people's bodies survive the Change, but their minds don't." His stepfather's face was serious. "Part of the reason I'm the alpha is that I can resist the pull of the moon longer than anyone else in this pack. If the moon sends you mad, I'll be here to deal with the consequences."

He drew the knife partway from the sheath, showing Garth the shining blade.

"Is that—?"

"Silver? Yes."

Holy shit. If he ended up a raving monster, his stepfather would only have to nick him with that blade and he'd be dead.

"That's kind of a dangerous thing to have around werewolves, isn't it?"

Kevin flashed a toothy smile that did nothing to reassure him. "That's the idea."

He felt the moon before he saw it: pain knifed into his guts and he staggered, nearly fell. His mother turned to him, a fierce grin on her face. Then the pain hit again and he did fall, dropping to the ground like a felled tree. A cry of shocked agony ripped from his throat.

The bones of his legs and arms cracked, sending sharp spikes of pain tearing through him. Dimly he was aware of other cries and hideous bone-crunching noises in the background, but his own pain focused his attention. He closed his eyes and screamed as his broken bones began to melt and reform themselves into new shapes. The pain was beyond anything he'd imagined.

He screamed, and heard his own voice change, coming out high-pitched and inhuman. He rolled on the coarse grass, as if he could force the pain from his body that way.

He was burning up, burning away. Every cell of his body was on fire. Soon there would be nothing left but ashes.

His muscles tore and regrew. He screamed till his throat was hoarse. What had he done? He was going to die. No one could endure this much pain and live. He would be one of those failures that didn't make it through the Change.

He felt his face deforming, the muscles of his jaw stretching, bone popping and cracking. God, if he was going to die, make it quick. He couldn't stand much more of this.

He lay, panting and whimpering, while a strange hissing sounded in his ears. The wind? He cracked one eyelid and saw hair sprouting—on his arm? No, it was a leg now. His heart pounded as adrenaline rushed through him. Was he—?

A wolf. It took a long moment to realise the pain had stopped; his nerve endings were still firing with remembered agony. Cautiously, the new wolf found his feet, staggering to an unfamiliar standing position on all fours. A man stood before him, the naked blade in his hand catching the first rays of moonlight. There was a wrongness about that blade that made the wolf whine uneasily.

He looked around; the small sheltering space between the boulders was filled with other wolves, stretching and sniffing each other. All watched him. The man watched him, too.

He stretched experimentally, head down, front paws out in front, his rump high in the air, feeling the stretch through unfamiliar limbs, all the way down to his clawed toes. Then he shook, feeling his fur ripple all the way from shoulders to tail. He felt powerful, ready to take on the world.

Ready to kill everything that moved.

He took a step toward the man. Hot blood ran through those veins, and he could spill it so easily. A growl rumbled through his chest.

A she-wolf stepped in front of the man and growled back. Her yellow eyes bored into him, and the bloodlust receded a little. She smelled like home. Mother.

She nudged him roughly, shoving her nose deep into the fur of his ruff, then nipped his ear hard enough to draw blood, reminding him she was more than just his mother. An overwhelming urge to submit took him, and he dropped immediately and showed her his pale belly. He felt her as a soothing presence in his mind, calming the raging need for blood. She stood over him a moment, as if to remind him she could tear his throat out if she wished.

The man sheathed his frightening blade and tore his clothes off. Then he fell to the ground and rose again, a midnight black wolf.

The wolf joined them. He growled, and the new wolf cringed. This was the alpha. His presence crashed into the new wolf's mind, demanding obedience. The big black wolf closed his jaws around the cringing wolf's neck, not hard enough to hurt, but enough to demonstrate his power. It was a reminder of the consequences of disobedience. These two were father and mother to the whole pack, but they could also be judge, jury, and executioner if necessary.

When the alpha released him, the new wolf scrambled to his feet, keeping his head bowed and eyes averted. The alpha pair stood one on each side of him, their flanks pressing against his, while the rest of the pack approached one by one. They smelled his scent, and he learned theirs, so that he would know them in the dark. Each one had that indefinable something that identified them as pack: a scent of home, of belonging, as well as their own individual smell.

The new wolf trembled as the parade continued. There were so many. His legs twitched with the urge to run, and his mouth filled with saliva. The hunt called to him, but the firm pressure of the alphas' bodies against his held him in place. The glowing disk of the moon cleared the trees, and he began to pant, his tongue lolling from his mouth. The black alpha growled a warning, but the moon's call was strong. The urge to obedience warred with his instincts. He wanted to rend and kill, feel the hot rush of blood in his mouth.

At last each member of the pack had greeted him, and the alpha lifted his snout and bayed at the moon. Released by this signal, the wolves streamed down the hill, tails held high, ears pricked. The new wolf ran with them, nose lifted to scent the air. The breeze told him many things: of kangaroos foraging among the trees, of possums and feral cats and other small prey. It wafted the dry, dusty scent of lizards and snakes to his questing nose, and something else, something that made his mouth water. The pack leader had caught that scent, too, and he changed direction, angling across the grass at the base of the hill.

The pack splashed through the small stream hard on his tail. They all had the scent now, and they moved with eagerness. On the far side of the stream they fanned out into a hunting formation, and slipped through the trees like ghosts, moving shadows in the night.

The moonlight painted the bush silver and grey, with deep black pools of darkness where the light couldn't reach. Everything was clear and hard-edged, almost bright as day to the wolf's eyes. His nose filled in the story, showing him where the other members of the pack were, and where their quarry lay. The mouth-watering scent of pig filled his nostrils as they followed it through the tall gums.

The wolf had no sense of time, but the moon was almost overhead when the pack slowed from their easy ground-eating lope to a trot. Up ahead lay a great swathe of bracken, the source of the tantalising scent. Several wolves split off and disappeared around the edges of the bracken, circling around behind the pig, while the rest waited patiently. The hunt wasn't to be rushed. Patience and perseverance were a hunter's greatest skills.

Suddenly a panicked squeal rent the night, followed by a crashing of bracken. Something big was moving through the fronds, which dipped and waved wildly as it passed. Swaying in the plants behind it showed the passage of several wolves, driving the creature before them.

The pig burst out of the bracken, almost under the wolf's very nose. It was a huge tusker, twice the size of the wolf, but he hurled himself at its throat all the same. His blood was up; he could taste that pig flesh already.

His teeth snapped closed on coarse pig hair as the hog twisted with surprising speed. One tusk gored a trail of fire all down his side. He yelped in pain and tried to relaunch himself at the charging animal, but his legs had lost their power, and his leap fell short.

It didn't matter. There was no escape for the pig. Three other wolves leapt on it and bore it to the ground. It squealed and kicked, lashing out with its tusks, but more wolves piled on, snapping and snarling. Its struggles weakened, then stopped altogether.

The snarling rose to a crescendo as the alpha stood over the kill, driving the other wolves back. Not till they had arranged themselves in an obedient circle round the pig's body did he drop his snout and tear a hunk of flesh free. In the moonlight it dripped black blood. The wolf could smell it from his place in the circle, rich and meaty. He whined as he watched the alpha feast, panting with the pain of his wound.

The alpha's mate joined him, and then the beta of the pack, a big grey wolf with a paler patch around his neck, taller than the alpha but not as solid. Once they'd finished they stepped back from the kill and watched as each pack member approached in turn, from highest to lowest.

The new wolf was last, held in place by the alpha's will. Delicious entrails steamed in the cold night air, taunting him as he watched the others feast. But at least the enforced wait gave his side time to begin healing. It wasn't a very deep gash, but it was long, and blood matted his fur all down that side. As he crouched, awaiting his turn, he could feel a strange crawling sensation as the edges of the wound came together and began to knit, and the pain started to recede.

At last the alpha glanced his way, and the wolf surged to his feet. There wasn't much left of the pig by then, but he tore into the bloody flesh, burying his snout in the carcass. Pure heaven burst into his mouth. It was the best meal he'd ever had, and he gobbled chunks of raw pig meat as if it was his last, determined to fill his belly before some more senior wolf chased him away.

***

The wolf could have run all night. Belly full of pig, the gash on his side just an aching memory, he felt the power of his shifter strength, his shifter muscles. Nothing could stop him. His veins zinged with energy. He leapt and gambolled among the bracken with two of the younger wolves, too restless to sit still.

When the alpha signalled it was time to head back to the den, the wolf bounded ahead, glad to stretch his legs. He startled a rabbit, and gave furious chase till the frightened bundle of fur found the safety of its hole. His nose sang to him of the pulsing life that filled the bush, and he wanted to chase everything. Eat everything.

The other wolves were moving fast, and he circled back to join them. They covered the distance back to the den much faster than they had come, now that they were no longer trying to disguise their presence from the prey. The bush was theirs, and they strode through it, proud owners of this land and all it contained.

Back across the stream they went, and up the bare rocky hill to their place among the boulders at the top. The wolves who hadn't joined the hunt—the pups and their carers—greeted them with licks and sniffs. Some of the older members of the pack regurgitated hunks of steaming meat, which the pups fell on with great delight, and everyone found a place to settle. There were still hours of darkness remaining, and time not spent either hunting or sleeping was time wasted according to a wolf's view of life.

The wolf sprawled in the heap of warm furry bodies with the others, but couldn't settle. His bloodlust had been sated by the hunt, but a scent teased his nostrils, a scent that promised everything his wolfish heart desired. It hinted at dark nights and warm pulsating bodies. It whispered of running free under the moon with one wolf who was more than just pack.

That scent belonged to the she-wolf with the dainty muzzle and the ruddy gold fur. He'd been vaguely aware of her all night, but the hunt had taken most of his attention until now. He shifted in the pile of bodies, squirming his way closer to her, ignoring the protests of sleepy wolves who snapped at him for disturbing their rest.

When at last he fetched up next to her he took a deep breath of that intoxicating scent. His heart beat faster as she turned to him, a question in her amber eyes. He nuzzled his face against hers.

She recoiled with a warning growl, which roused the wolf on her other side. He rose to his feet, the white ruff of his hackles standing up, and growled in unmistakeable challenge. The wolf rose, too, ready for anything. Whatever it took to win the red-gold wolf, and prove himself a worthy mate.

But she stood at the white-ruffed wolf's side, shoulder to shoulder with him. The message was clear. *This is the mate I have chosen.*

The wolf felt a hollowness open in his belly. But he could still challenge. He would show her she had chosen wrong. Already he felt a deep hatred for the white-ruffed wolf, standing there so confident of his place. He would bring this rival down, and then the beautiful one would turn to him. He snarled, and gathered himself for a spring.

He didn't even see the alpha coming. The first thing he knew, he was on his back in the dirt, the alpha's jaws snapping in his face, all hot breath and spittle. The alpha pinned him with his weight till he showed his belly in submission. The urge to fight for the red-gold wolf was strong, but the instinct to cower before the alpha was stronger. As he lay there he watched the red-gold wolf and her mate settle down again, bodies curled around each other.

He whined, and the alpha let him up, but when he would have rejoined the pile of sleeping bodies, the pack leader barred his way. Rejected, he slunk off and curled up near the entrance to the cave where the youngest members of the pack slept.

When he woke the rising sun dazzled his eyes, and the smell of bacon cooking started his stomach growling. He'd just started a long, luxurious stretch when something whacked him in the face. Startled, he jerked upright, only to find it was his own clothes, and he was lying there buck naked.

"Better get those on," his mother said. She was already dressed in jeans, hiking boots and a warm jacket. Her breath puffed in the chilly air as she spoke. "You'll cool down fast now you've lost your fur. Breakfast is nearly ready if you want it."

He dressed quickly, horribly conscious that he was the last one naked. Mum and some of the more senior wolves had probably been human for a couple of hours. How many people had seen him stretched out here in the buff? Not that any of them would have cared, but he did. A man liked his privacy—especially from his mother.

"I'm starving," he said, and he was, which seemed strange. He vaguely remembered gorging himself on wild pig last night.

"That's probably because you got yourself injured in the hunt. Shifter healing is miraculous, but it takes a lot of fuel. How are you feeling this morning?"

"Fine." He'd forgotten the injury. He lifted his shirt now and found nothing but a thin white line to show where the pig's tusk had scored him.

"That'll fade," his mother said. "This time next week, there'll be nothing to show for last night's adventures."

Last night's adventures. They were a blur of motion now, of running through the darkened bush, of fur catching on twigs, rocks turning beneath his padded feet. Sounds and smells, bloody red flesh tearing beneath his teeth, the white flash of a rabbit's tail, the thrill of the chase …

The way the red-gold wolf's lip had twisted into a snarl when he approached her.

He wished he didn't remember that. He looked around now for Carly. His wolf mind had no use for names, but he knew who the red-gold wolf was. If he tried, he could still smell her. She smelled of lazy summer afternoons and hot summer nights, of fur and sex and flowers. She was at the campfire, standing close to its warmth, with Rhys at her side. As he watched she turned her face up to Rhys and laughed at something he'd said, her auburn hair flowing like living flame down her back.

"Wolves mate for life, you know," his mother said.

He dragged his eyes away from Carly. "We're not wolves. We're humans."

"You *were* human, you stupid boy. Then you got your brother to bite you. Now you're a shifter. A werewolf. But not a true one, according to some. You're only moonborn, not wolfborn."

He shrugged. Why did she have to go into this now, with the whole sharp-eared pack around? "Same thing."

She made an exasperated sound. "You are so like your father. Stubborn as they come. It's *not* the same thing. How can you have grown up surrounded by the pack and not seen that? Have you had your eyes shut all these years? We moonborn are second-class citizens. Why didn't you tell me what you were thinking of doing?"

Because you would have tried to stop me? That one was so obvious he didn't have to say it.

He folded his arms across his broad chest defensively. His mother had a knack for making him feel about five years old. "You seem to have done all right for a second-class citizen. You're the alpha's mate."

"That's because *he* chose *me*. I would have been the lowest of the low otherwise." She dropped her voice. "And watch how fast I slide down the ranks if he ever changes his mind. I'll have skid marks on my backside."

There was little chance of that. Kevin doted on Mum, always had, as long as Garth could remember. In fact he was watching her now from the other side of the fire. He kept glancing across, as if to assure himself she was there, while he spoke to his beta. They'd always been a close couple. That was the kind of connection Garth wanted for himself.

His mother followed the direction of his gaze. Carly was just the other side of Kevin and Sean.

"Wolves are obsessed with rank. Particularly the born ones." She sighed. "You don't know what you've let yourself in for. And our little red-headed friend is just as bad as the others. Why do you think she's stuck so close to that idiot Rhys all these years? Do you think he'd be so attractive if his father wasn't pack beta?"

She shouldn't talk about Carly that way. "You make it sound like we're animals. But we're human ninety-eight per cent of the time."

She laughed, though it was a bitter sound. "The wolf is always there, just under the skin. You'll find yourself acting in ways you never did before, feeling things you've never felt. Mad impulses. The hardest part of being a new wolf is not giving into them. The wolf rules us."

"But we don't mate for life," he insisted. "I've seen plenty of people change partners."

"Yes. But when we're in wolf form, we follow wolf rules. It's instinct. You try coming between a mated pair and they'll both tear you apart. You were lucky."

"Can we talk about this some other time?" *Like maybe, never?* He felt sure the whole pack was listening.

His mother rolled on as if he hadn't spoken, though she did lower her voice. "Even in human form, the urge to preserve the bond is very strong. Yes, sometimes a couple will break up. But it's hard, much harder than for regular humans. It goes against our nature."

"Thanks for the tip. I think I'll have some of that bacon now."

He strode towards the campfire, desperate to escape the conversation. His brother was there, with little Mac, both tucking into huge helpings of bacon and greasy fried eggs.

"I'm glad you didn't die," said Mac, in her piping childish voice.

"Mac!" Mac's mother looked up from her own plate, scandalised.

"What? I *am* glad he didn't die."

"Me, too." Garth grinned at her. Kids had no filters. They just said whatever came into their heads. He liked that about them. You always knew where you stood. If they wanted something, they said so. No bullshit.

"How was the hunt?" Trevor asked. Interest warred with resentment in his expression, since he hadn't been allowed to join the hunt, penned in the den with the other juveniles.

Garth shoved half a rasher of bacon into his mouth. Its greasy goodness exploded on his tongue with an intensity he'd never experienced before.

"It was ..." How did he describe it? Running free, slipping through the shadows like a shadow himself while the wind brought him a thousand stories of the life all around him, cowering in the dark as the predators passed.

The final exhilarating rush, the fear as the boar charged him, the red-hot pain as its tusk caught him, and then at last, the taste of its flesh as he tore into it, blood coating his muzzle.

"It was good," he said.

His brother gave him a disgusted look.

"When I'm grown up," said Mac, "I'm going to lead the hunt and catch fifty kangaroos."

"What are you going to do with fifty kangaroos?" Garth asked.

"Eat them, of course."

"Then you'll be so fat you won't be able to move."

"She'll explode," Trevor said. "There'll be bits of Mac guts everywhere, hanging from the trees like ugly pink ropes."

Mac wrinkled her freckled nose. "I will not. That's disgusting." She thought about it some more. "Well, then, I'll share them with the rest of the pack. That's what packs are for, aren't they? We share with each other. And you'll probably be too old to hunt for yourself by then, so you'll need me to take care of you."

Trevor laughed. "You know I'm only ten years older than you, right?"

She nodded, as if he'd just proved her point. Seventeen must seem pretty old when you were only seven. What must she think of him, then? At twenty-two, he must be practically at retirement age.

Carly's musical laugh caught his attention, and he glanced across the fire to where she lounged next to Rhys and Jensen. To her, he was just a kid, though she was only a few years older. When she saw Garth watching her, she caught Rhys's grease-smeared face in her hand and planted a long, slow kiss on him.

Well, that was pretty clear. He looked down at the food still on his plate and felt sick. The greasy weight of what he'd already eaten lay like bacon-flavoured concrete in the bottom of his stomach. She had no interest in him. His mother was right. The red-gold wolf had claimed her mate and it wasn't him.

He was the world's biggest idiot. He'd become a wolf, given up his humanity, and it made no difference. She still didn't want him.

SEVENTH MOON

He'd borrowed a ute from a friend at the gym, and the tray was already more than half-full with boxes. Just as well the skies were clear today, though the new apartment wasn't far.

His brother came down the front steps, lumping a heavy box of books as if it were packed full of cotton wool. Removalist would be a good profession for a werewolf. Not that gym instructor was a bad one. Garth had so many clients clamouring for his personal attention these days he was thinking of starting up his own business.

The ute's tray bounced as Trevor dropped the heavy box in. "How many Star Wars novelisations does one man need?"

"That's a stupid question." Garth grinned at his brother, who'd filled out a little in the months since he turned eighteen. "All of them, of course."

"I've never seen the attraction, myself. They're just movies. There are plenty of better ones out there."

"Wash your mouth out, boy. Are you blaspheming against the great god Lucas?"

"Ha. The great god Lucas can't write dialogue to save his life."

"Impudent you are. Punish you I will."

Garth seized his brother in a headlock, but Trevor soon managed to wrestle his way free. Garth's new werewolf muscles, however much they impressed the girls at the gym, were still no match for those of his scrawny brother. Bloody wolfborn. No wonder they lorded it over moonborn like him. He scowled as his brother bounded away up the stairs to the front deck and disappeared into the house.

Well, no use brooding about it. That was why he was moving out, to get away from the constant jabs and sneers. It would be heaven to have his own place and not have to put up with the pack descending en masse every bloody weekend. Heaven not to have put up with Rhys "accidentally" bumping into him all the time, testing his strength. Always so happy to find that he was still stronger.

And, if he was honest, it would be pretty damn good not to have to see Carly any more, except at full moon. Her attitude had changed since he'd been turned. She'd gone from treating him with a patronising fondness, as if he were a little kid, to barely acknowledging his presence.

Sometimes when he spoke to her she stared right through him as if he wasn't there. He didn't need that kind of shit in his life.

He stared down at the box of books, unseeing. If only he'd thought it through. It had seemed like a good idea at the time, but now he was stuck as a goddamn werewolf for the rest of his life, and once a month he had to run through the bush with the pack, his blood up, and know that the red-gold wolf would never look his way.

Seemed like a good idea at the time. Huh. He should get that tattooed on his arm. It was practically his motto. His life seemed to be littered with impulsive moves that had turned out wrong.

However, this wouldn't be one of them. He couldn't wait to get away from the competitive, insular world of the pack house. With a bit of luck he could forget all about them except at full moon.

He was halfway up the wooden stairs when he heard a car pull up, and a woman's voice called out to him.

"Deb!" He hurried back down the stairs. "What are you doing here?"

She slammed the car door and strode across the grass. She wore denim shorts so short they left nothing to the imagination, showing off the tanned muscles of her long legs. Those muscles had cost hours of effort in the gym; he knew because he'd supervised quite a few of them.

She tossed her ponytail carelessly over one shoulder. Her hair was red, almost the same glowing shade as Carly's, though he suspected Deb's came out of a bottle.

"Thought I'd come and give you a hand with the move."

"I didn't even know you knew where I lived."

She shrugged, and ran her gaze over the contents of the ute. They'd been out a couple of times. He'd kissed her after their last date, and she certainly seemed interested enough. But she was part of his other life, the clean, uncomplicated one that didn't include supernatural creatures and their power struggles, and he was very keen to keep it that way. He glanced up at the house, hoping that no one had noticed her arrival.

"Is this it?" She gestured at the boxes. "No fridge? No microwave or TV?"

"I've already moved that stuff in. This is the last of it."

She moved closer and kissed his cheek, enveloping him in a wave of perfume. Of course Trevor chose that moment to appear, toting another box, followed by their mother.

Deb greeted the new arrivals cheerfully. "Hi, I'm Deb."

Trevor dumped the box in with the others and gave the shorts an appreciative look. "I'm Trevor."

"He's my brother," Garth said. "And this is my mum, Carol."

"Hello, Deb." His mother smiled, but she stopped halfway down the stairs. She'd been a wolf nearly half her life, an alpha's mate, and assuming a position of dominance came as naturally to her as breathing. Even if she was only moonborn. "Nice to meet you."

Deb said hello and leaned back against the ute, crossing her arms under her breasts, which drew Trevor's eyes.

"Is that the last one?" Garth asked, and Trevor jerked his gaze away and nodded.

Garth was more of a leg man. From the shorts it looked like Deb had figured that out already.

"In that case, I'll help you unpack at the other end," said Deb.

"Really, you don't need to do that." He could feel the approaching full moon like an itch under his skin. Not a good time for her to choose to drop in.

And that was the moment Rhys rocketed his souped-up Holden into the driveway, blocking the ute in. He and Carly got out, and the two red-headed women eyed each other warily.

"Another brother?" Deb asked.

"No." Thank God. "Just a friend of the family."

Which wasn't exactly true, but he could hardly introduce him as a member of the pack, though it grated him to apply the word "friend" in any way to Rhys Donohue.

"You're going to have to move that heap of yours," he called to Rhys. "I'm just about to leave."

Rhys muttered something that could have been "good riddance" but he made no move to get back in his car. "Where's your furniture? You going to sleep on the floor? Or you going to be be spending your nights somewhere else?"

He winked at Deb, who coloured slightly.

"Gosh, Rhys, I didn't know you cared." He'd have liked to punch that smug face, but that had never worked out well for him in the past. He clenched his fists and then tried to make it look as if he hadn't. Even an impulsive guy could figure out that starting a fistfight in front of his mother and his very new girlfriend wasn't the greatest idea. "Are you going to miss me?"

His mother cut in before Rhys could reply, a weary tone in her voice. "Just move your car, Rhys."

Rhys threw her a surly look, but he got back in the car and started it up. The engine grumbled to life, and he backed out and parked in the street while Carly sauntered up the driveway, her hips swinging in a hypnotic rhythm. She wore jeans, but Garth knew that underneath her legs were every bit as long and toned as Deb's. God knew he'd seen them, and everything else she had on display, often enough. Werewolves were the world's original nudists.

She brushed past him without speaking and climbed the stairs to the deck. He stared after her with that longing that never seemed to go away. He dragged his eyes away from that denim-clad backside swaying up the stairs and found his mother watching him. She looked pointedly at Deb, who was still leaning against the back of the ute, and he scowled.

"You have a definite 'type', don't you?" she murmured as she came down the stairs and joined him. "You might find it easier to focus on one girl at a time, though."

He ignored the comment. "I'd better head off. Got a lot of unpacking to do."

His mother looked past him to the red-haired girl lounging against the ute. "Just don't get too wrapped up in her."

"I've barely started going out with her, Mum."

"As long as you realise—you can't have a serious relationship with her."

"Why not?"

"How are you going to hide it from her, every full moon? You can't tell her."

"If it comes to that, I'll think of something. Relax, would you?" He kissed her on the cheek and went to join Deb.

"I'll follow you there, shall I?" she asked, smiling at him.

She really did look a lot like Carly, though her eyes were brown where Carly's were blue, and the shape of her face was more rounded. When she smiled at him like that his heart kind of sped up in his chest. Other parts of his anatomy started to stir, too.

"You don't need to do that." He took her arm and urged her down the drive toward her car. Her skin was soft beneath his fingers. "I can unpack a few boxes without help. I'm sure you've got better things to do on a Sunday afternoon."

And besides, the moon would rise when the sun went down, and he'd have to be miles away with the pack by then.

"I can't think of anything I'd rather do with the afternoon than spend it with you."

The look in her eyes made him catch his breath. She'd lowered her voice, but he knew that Mum and Trevor would have heard her anyway. Werewolf ears were sharp. He didn't look back as he marched her down the drive. Trevor's face would be a picture.

At least Rhys wasn't listening. He was on his mobile, leaning his elbows on the roof of his car while he talked. He'd parked so close behind Deb's car their bumper bars were almost touching.

Toby from next door bounded out to bark as they neared his fence. Toby took the fact that there were werewolves living next door as a personal insult, and never missed an opportunity to announce his disapproval, though he always made sure to do it from a safe distance. He was only a little dog, but Deb screamed when he appeared, and shrank back behind Garth.

"Don't worry about Toby. He won't hurt you." But she stood rooted to the spot. "Are you okay? You're shaking."

"I don't like dogs." Her tanned face had lost its colour. She watched the little dog as if terrified that he might spring at her any minute. "Can you … make him go away?"

Garth growled and Toby's ears lost their jaunty stance and flattened against his head. He stopped barking. Garth took a menacing step toward him and Toby fled for the safety of his own front porch.

Deb scuttled around her car and unlocked the driver's door. Her hand was still shaking. Her eyes met his over the car's roof.

"Thanks. I got attacked by a dog when I was little. I've never liked them since."

A snort of laughter behind them revealed that Rhys was off the phone.

"That's understandable." Garth's temper began to rise, but he kept his eyes on Deb and tried to ignore the idiot.

Deb's cheeks flushed a delicate pink. "Is he laughing at me?"

Garth gritted his teeth. "Must have been a funny phone call."

"People shouldn't let their dogs run wild like that." She shot a cool glance at Rhys, then got in her car. "Call me."

She waved out the window and took off. No more talk of following him or helping him unpack, or whatever it was she'd been offering. That was probably a good thing, considering the moon. Garth took a deep breath and headed back to his car.

"Hey, Trev!" Rhys shouted. "Did you see that? Garth's new girl is scared of dogs."

Garth slammed the ute's door, but the revving of the engine couldn't drown out the sound of Rhys's mocking laughter.

FOURTEENTH MOON
One year a werewolf

Garth pulled into his parking space underneath the apartment block, got out and stretched. Joints popped, as if they weren't quite used to their human configuration yet. He always felt odd after shifting, not quite fully in his skin again. Deb's car was parked in one of the visitor's spots outside, he noticed as he walked to the stairs. The body corporate would be complaining again, like last month, but the local teenagers had taken to smashing windscreens of cars left out on the street, so what could they do? The unit only came with one car space.

Maybe he should go hunting one night and teach the stupid kids to avoid this street. The thought brought a smile to his lips as he entered the apartment.

Deb was up already, though it wasn't even eight o'clock. Unusual for a Saturday, especially since she'd had Janie's party last night.

She was sitting at the table, nursing a cup of coffee. He stopped behind her and dropped a kiss on her bright red hair. She smelled of sunshine and kisses and something floral.

"Morning. You're up early. You okay?"

"I'm fine." She toyed with the handle of her coffee mug and didn't look up.

She looked beat.

"Must have been one hell of a party."

"It was fine."

He paused, about to head for the shower. Something about her flat tone wasn't right.

"Fine? Is everything fine this morning?"

She looked up at him, and there was a flinty look in those normally soft brown eyes. "Actually, no."

"What's wrong?"

"Nothing. How was your night?"

Women. Why couldn't they just say what they meant? He felt a flash of temper, and the snark just slipped out. "My night was fine, too."

He knew he wasn't reacting right. But there was an accusation in that look, and he knew he hadn't done anything. What was her problem?

"Did you stay over at Trevor's?"

"Yes."

"That's odd." Her tone was deliberate. "Janie made some throwaway comment as I was leaving about how often you seem to disappear. It got me thinking, so I drove past Trevor's on the way home, and your car wasn't there. There were no cars there at all, and none of the lights were on. It looked like no one was home. Were you playing cards in the dark?"

He hesitated. Fatal mistake. He opened his mouth but she cut him off.

"Don't lie to me, Garth. I know you weren't playing cards with your brother and his mates, so where were you?"

Shit. What should he say? *I was running through the state forest chasing a deer* wasn't going to cut it. "We decided to go out for drinks instead. Went down to the pub and played some pool. We didn't get back till late."

"How late?"

"I don't know, I didn't check my watch. I was pretty drunk by then."

"Three o'clock? Four o'clock?"

"Probably three o'clock. I don't know. Why does it matter what time it was?"

"Because I sat outside that house all night. I only beat you home by an hour. You weren't there."

He rubbed a hand over his face, feeling the stubble there. This was bad. He was helpless under her furious, wounded gaze. He wanted to take her in his arms and kiss that look away, but that clearly wasn't an option. What could he say?

"Who is she?"

"Who?"

"The girl you're seeing. Is is someone from the gym? Irene? You seem to spend a lot of time with her lately."

"Irene? Whoa, hang on there. Where are you getting this stuff from? Irene's just a client. I'm not seeing anyone. I'm with you."

She ignored him. "Is it that girl that's always hanging around at your mum's place, then? Carly or Cathy or whatever her name is?"

"No! God, no. Honey, I'm not seeing anyone, I swear." He tried to draw her to her feet, but she wouldn't budge from her seat.

"Then where were you? The truth this time."

The truth? He ran a hand through his hair, feeling hot, nervous sweat break out under his arms and across his face. The truth? That was the last thing she wanted to hear, this sweet sunlit girl who was afraid of dogs. She didn't even like puppies, and who the hell doesn't like puppies? How was he supposed to tell her that her boyfriend was a goddamn werewolf?

Every minute he kept silent was another layer deeper in the shit. Her face was closing up, shutting him out. But he couldn't think what else to say. He was at work? She knew as well as he did the gym didn't stay open all night. Why couldn't he have one of those jobs where he had to travel interstate to meetings all the time? Then it would have been easy to cover full moon. Last month he'd told her he was going to Adelaide to meet up with an old friend. The month before he'd supposedly run over a dog and had to take it to an all-night vet. He was a terrible liar. Having to come up with something every month to cover his necessary absence was killing him.

And it obviously hadn't worked anyway. Tears stood in her big brown eyes. He sat in the chair next to her and took her hands, though she tried to pull them away. What could he say now that she would believe? Nothing. He might as well try the truth. It would be so good to have it out in the open, instead of having to hide this part of himself from her.

"I don't think you're going to like the truth."

Her fingers quivered in his. She stared him straight in the eye. "Whatever it is, it will be better than being lied to."

"Okay." He swallowed hard. There was really no way to lead up to something like this gently. "I'm a—" Shit. He tried again. "I'm a werewolf."

He'd never been much good at gentle anyway.

She snatched her hands away, the hurt on her face replaced by fury.

"Oh, for *God's* sake!"

She slammed her chair back and stalked away. He followed her.

"It's true. It was full moon last night. I can't be around people at full moon."

"Or what? You'll eat them?" She threw him a look of such disgust he caught his breath. "Grow up, Garth."

"It's true!"

She folded her arms. "Fine. Show me then. Change into a werewolf."

"I can't do it now. It's day time!"

"Oh, that's convenient, isn't it? And I suppose you can only change at full moon, too, so I'll have to wait until next month to see, will I?"

He felt helpless under the onslaught of her rage. "No, I can change any night if I want to. But at full moon I have to. It's a compulsion."

"Well, let's make a date then, shall we? You and me, tonight, so I can meet your alter ego."

"I really don't think that's a good idea." *You don't even like dogs.* What would she think of the black wolf? He was a big, mean-looking bastard. Belatedly, he remembered he wasn't supposed to tell anyone who wasn't a shifter about his other side. The dragons got shitty with shifters who spilled the beans on their secret world. Shitty enough for some shifters who'd done so to disappear.

"Why? Do I look so appetising that you'll jump on me and eat me the minute you grow fur and fangs?"

"Don't joke about it. On full moon night I would. It's a kind of madness. I can hardly even remember what I've done when I wake up the next day." She was looking at him as if he'd grown an extra head. "But you'd be safe tonight. I can pretty much stay in control any other night." Pretty much.

"Fine. It's a date then."

There was that word again. Fine. Nothing about this seemed fine to him, but what was the alternative? He'd gone this far. He had to try to convince her. She'd only moved in three months ago, but it had been the best three months of his life. He couldn't imagine life without her now. Maybe they could still work this out.

***

He had a few clients lined up at the gym. He worked alongside them all, working those werewolf muscles hard, pushing himself. Trying to forget the mess he'd made. Mum had told him relationships outside the pack didn't work, and this was why. So much for proving her wrong.

Deb wasn't answering her mobile. Who knew where she'd gone, or whether she'd be back?

He was relieved, when he got home, to find her clothes still hanging in the wardrobe beside his. Surely that was a good sign. Maybe when she'd calmed down they could talk about this like reasonable human beings. Or like one reasonable human being and one werewolf, anyway. It was no use now trying to come up with some lie to cover his absences. He'd have to stick with the truth and hope she was one of those rare humans that adjusted all right to the news that there were shapeshifters living among them.

Trying not to dwell on the dismal odds of that, he showered and put on his faded blue shirt, the one she liked because she said it brought out the blue in his eyes. Most people thought they were grey, but whatever. He'd try anything. Then he sat, flicking through TV channels and seeing none of them, waiting for her to come home.

What would he do if she didn't? He knew where some of her friends lived; he supposed he could try some of them. Maybe she'd run to Janie, or Emma. Her parents lived in Adelaide, so she wouldn't have gone to them. Not if she meant to keep her job, at least.

When at last he heard her key in the lock he jumped up, weak with relief.

"I wasn't sure if you'd come back." He moved toward her, but she sidestepped him and went straight into the bedroom, where she tugged a suitcase down off the top shelf and began to throw clothes into it.

"Please don't do this." Watching shirts and dresses tumble into the case made him feel sick. "I don't want you to go."

"Well, that's just a shame, isn't it?" She focused on shoving her clothes into the case, crumpling them into careless piles, and didn't look at him. "Because I don't want to stay with someone I can't trust." Now she looked at him, and he wished she hadn't. Fury still smouldered in those brown eyes. "Someone who isn't even man enough to own up to what he's done. You could at least tell me who she is, instead of making up this crap about werewolves."

"It's not crap." He pulled the shirt off over his head in one swift, frustrated movement, then started unbuckling his belt.

"What are you doing?" She paused, arms full of dresses. "I am *not* having sex with you."

He kicked off his shoes, slid out of his jeans. "Watch this."

He reached for the wolf. It always hovered close beneath the surface, and this was getting easier every time he did it. Sometimes that worried him; would the wolf one day take over, and he would lose his humanity completely? But this wasn't one of those times. He felt the warmth of change flooding him and cried out in pain and relief.

She backed away as he dropped to the floor, the music of breaking bones loud in his ears. The pain was exquisite, though nothing like the nightmare of the first time. He whimpered at the agony of his face reforming, the bone and muscles stretching and rearranging themselves. Too hard to concentrate on anything else as his body remade itself, but he heard her scream. It sounded like it came from a long way away.

When he rose to all fours, the woman was out of the bedroom and halfway to the door of the apartment, sobbing in terror. He sprang across the room and knocked her down. He couldn't quite remember why, but he knew he didn't want her to leave. Didn't want to hurt her either, though she smelled good. Smelled familiar somehow. Sunshine and flowers and—? His mate, that was it, when he was in that other, two-legged form.

She covered her face and sobbed. He licked her cheek and tasted salt. Time to go.

He endured the change a second time, somehow managing to keep hold of her as he writhed. He felt as limp as a wet sock when he came to himself; changing twice in a row so quickly drained him terribly. But he needed words now, and the wolf couldn't help with words.

"Deb," he whispered. "It's okay. It's just me." He rolled off her. "See? Back to normal."

Still she sobbed, and refused to move her hands. In the end he had to pry them away from her face and coax her off the floor. He led her back to the bedroom and sat her on the bed next to the half-full suitcase so he could put his clothes back on. He was starting to acquire a certain shifter carelessness about nudity, after a year as a wolf, but this was not the time to present himself as anything less than fully human.

She sat quietly while he dressed, but as soon as he sat down beside her on the bed she screeched and leapt up.

"Don't come near me! You're a freak! A monster!"

So much for his hope that she might have an easy adjustment. "Maybe. But I'm still Garth, the same guy you fell in love with. The guy you wanted to move in with. We eat Chinese takeaway on Friday nights, we love going to the gym together, and sitting up late watching old movies. You hate my collection of Star Wars figures, but you don't hate me. We love each other, Deb. That hasn't changed."

She backed away, toward the bedroom door. "I told Janie what you said. She thought it was funny. Said at least you had a more creative excuse than the last cheating bastard."

Oh, shit. "You told Janie I'm a werewolf?"

"Yes." Her face crumpled and she started crying again, big gasping sobs that distorted her pretty face. "But I never thought it was true."

Her sobs tore at his heart and he tried to take her in his arms, but she screamed and leapt back.

"Deb, please! It's all right. I'm not going to hurt you."

He couldn't think. What should he do? She was going to run straight back to Janie and blurt out the whole story. The state she was in, Janie might even believe her. And then he was well and truly screwed. He couldn't have her spreading the word about him, not while she was this worked up—but he couldn't see any way to calm her down.

Trevor. His little brother would know what to do. He was always so calm and logical, and there was no one else to turn to.

"Who are you calling?" She looked at him with such fear in her eyes it nearly broke his heart.

"Stay there." He shut the bedroom door behind him and stood in the tiny hallway with his back to the door. He could hardly tell her he was calling Trevor; it didn't take a genius to figure out that if Garth was a werewolf his brother probably was, too. Luckily Trevor picked up on the first ring.

"I need help. Can you come over?"

"Now? I'm studying for exams." Trevor wanted to be an accountant, or maybe a stockbroker. Anything, as long as it used his love of maths. He took his studying seriously. "What's the problem?"

Garth told him.

"Shit. I'll be right there."

***

Half an hour later Garth was on the road. Trevor was watching Deb until he came home. The scene as he was leaving was every bit as bad as he'd feared. He'd actually had to threaten Deb. The shame of that still burned.

"You can't keep me here!" Her voice had risen until she was almost screaming. He had the TV up loud, but he knew it was only a matter of time before the neighbours came knocking at this rate.

And that he couldn't allow, for all their sakes. The shifters were ruled by the dragon queens. The local queen's power made a pack alpha look like a child, and she was intent on keeping the shifter world hidden. She had never hesitated in the past to kill shifters who had revealed their trueshapes to humans, even accidentally. He knew he would be no exception. Deb herself would disappear, and probably Trevor, too.

"Yes, I can," he growled, allowing his wolf to surge closer to the surface. He knew it made his eyes glow golden, and she shrank away from him. "You'll stay here and keep quiet until I get back."

He hated to see the fear on her face.

"Or what?" she asked.

"What do you think?"

He let her imagination fill in the blanks, disgusted at himself. Now he was threatening his own girlfriend. How had he screwed this up so badly?

"Be quick," Trevor said, looking nervous at the prospect of standing guard over Deb. And Trevor wasn't even the one dealing with the goblins. "The chief and his hangers-on will probably be at the casino already. You might have better luck dealing with someone a bit lower down the food chain."

It had been Trevor's idea to go to the goblins. Through their mages, they had access to all kinds of useful spells, from simple love potions to spells that would allow the user to take on the exact appearance of someone else. Garth had even heard they could create changelings—a complete and exact copy of a living person—though he was never sure if he should believe the wilder stories about them. Probably the goblins made up some of the more impressive stuff just to make themselves look good, and to justify the high prices they charged. The wolves tended to leave them well alone, so Garth hadn't had much personal experience with them. He'd seen them about sometimes, of course. They looked as human as anyone else in their human guises, but there was no disguising that distinctive goblin scent from a sensitive werewolf nose. A scrawny young goblin with flame-coloured hair used to work at the supermarket across from the gym, though Garth hadn't seen him for a couple of years. He'd always chosen another checkout line when the goblin was working, preferring to keep his distance.

That didn't mean he didn't know how to find them, though. The whole clan had recently moved to one of those gated communities that had just been built in the affluent northern suburbs, so that was where he was going now.

Sooner than he would have liked, he was pulling up outside. He didn't trust goblins, but what choice did he have? How else was he going to make Deb forget what he'd told her, without a magic potion? Surely if the goblin mages could manage a potion to make a person fall in love with someone, they could manage a simple bit of forgetting.

He slammed his car door and stood in the street for a moment, sniffing the story that the breeze told him. He knew the scent of goblins: earthy, like rotting vegetation. They smelled of dark places and things buried deep, not the clean scent of the wind in the trees that he associated with wolves. One on one a goblin was no match for a wolf, but his nose told him there were many, many goblins here. The smell of them made the hairs on the back of his neck stand up and he almost got straight back in his car and drove off.

Don't be such a bloody sook. You made this mess; now get in there and clean it up.

The gate was locked, but there was an intercom system.

"Yes?" said a bored voice when he pressed the button.

"I'd like to talk to someone about buying a potion," he said.

"Name?"

"Garth Maclaren."

"Trueshape?"

"Wolf."

There was a long pause, presumably as the goblin went off to consult with someone. Eventually the gate unlocked with a click, and swung soundlessly open.

"Enter. Proceed to Number 13."

Well, there was an auspicious number. He passed through the gate and it closed behind him. No one was on the street. He could have driven in, but he felt too uneasy to be trapped in a car. He needed to be out in the open, free to act.

His boots hitting the pavement was the only sound. Though most of the houses showed lights in the windows, he might have been the only one here. But he knew he wasn't; he felt the pressure of eyes on the back of his skull, and had to fight the urge to spin around in search of the silent watchers. The hairs on the back of his neck prickled, and he swallowed a snarl.

Calm down, it's only goblins.

That scrawny young guy in the supermarket hadn't been too intimidating. A strong breeze could have knocked him over, and his eyes were always shifting, refusing to meet a challenge, like one who knows his place is way down at the bottom of the totem pole. Garth had never seen a goblin that radiated the sense of strength and threat that even the most junior wolf did, though admittedly he'd never met a mage. They were supposed to be plenty powerful.

But there was just something about them—a slyness, something in their manner that always made him wary. As if they always hovered one quick knife thrust away from betrayal.

He found Number 13, a narrow two-storey townhouse nestled up against its neighbours, no different from any of the others in the complex. He'd expected something a little grander, if this was where the mage lived. The porch light shone a welcome, but Garth hesitated on the doorstep. It didn't matter what he thought of goblins. They could supply what he needed. It was a business transaction, nothing more. He squared his shoulders and raised a hand to knock.

A young woman wearing a suspicious frown and the shortest dress he'd ever seen opened the door. She stank of goblin.

"You the one wanting a potion?"

"Yes."

She waved him into a small lounge room. "Wait here."

She left the room, shutting the door behind her. His sharp wolf hearing followed her footsteps to the back of the house, and caught the sound of conversation, though he couldn't hear the words. Then a different set of footsteps approached, heavier and more purposeful.

The goblin who entered the room wore a silk dressing gown, patterned in outrageous purple lilies, that strained to cover his generous belly.

"Forgive me," he said, lowering his bulk into an armchair opposite Garth. "I was just getting ready to go out. You're lucky you caught me at home."

Garth had never seen a fat goblin before. They tended to be thin, driven by nervous energy. Maybe this one was a mage—maybe that was where his air of assurance came from.

"They said you're a wolf. Are you here on behalf of the pack?"

"No. My name's—"

The goblin stopped him with a pudgy upraised hand. "No names necessary. The Chief isn't here at the moment, but I am authorised to negotiate for him in his absence. The gate says you're looking for a potion. What kind?"

"The kind to make somebody forget something."

The goblin's eyebrows drew together. "I'm afraid we can't make somebody forget something in particular without affecting the rest of their memory."

"Can you make them forget the last few hours, then?"

"Certainly. That's relatively simple. How many hours do you need?"

"Say the last twenty-four?"

"Excellent." The goblin clasped his chubby hands in his lap. Rings sparkled on every sausage-like finger. "The fee for that will be four thousand dollars."

"Four thousand—? But you said it was simple."

"It is simple. For a mage with years of training. That doesn't mean it's cheap."

In other words, there were no other options, so if you needed their magic, you had to pay whatever exorbitant price they asked.

"I don't have four thousand dollars. I barely have one."

The goblin rose from his seat. "Then I'm afraid our discussion is at an end. We do not barter. Four thousand is the price, take it or leave it."

Garth rose, too, frustration buzzing under his skin. Could he borrow money from Trevor? No. What was he thinking? The kid wouldn't have that kind of money stashed away.

"I guess I'll leave it then."

He stalked to the front door and let himself out into the night. The moon was up, just past full, and he felt it pull at his anger, tempting him to run wild, to taste blood. To fix problems with his teeth instead of his mind.

Except that was what had gotten him into this mess in the first place. He blew out a deep breath. What was he going to do now?

He headed back to the gate, turning over options in his mind. Ask Mum for the money? She'd be horrified, and there'd be hell to pay, but she'd probably help him if the alternative was his slip-up being discovered by the dragons. Could he break into the mage's house and steal what he needed? But he didn't even know what he was looking for.

As he passed the last house before the gate, a twig snapped among the azalea bushes and he stopped, searching the darkness for a threat. A head popped out from around the corner of the house.

"Psst. Over here."

Cautiously he left the path and skirted around the garden. The goblin was alone, and he backed into the darkness between the houses, beckoning Garth to follow until they were both hidden from view.

"Hey, I know you," Garth said. "You're that guy from the supermarket." Even in the dark he couldn't mistake the goblin's distinctive mop of orange hair.

"Yeah, not any more. I've come into my magic, so no more leaving the compound for Blue."

"You're a mage?" It was hard to keep the disbelief from his voice. Blue wore clothes that were none too clean, and he looked like he hadn't had a decent feed for a while. Surely a goblin mage would cut more of an imposing figure? More like the fat guy Garth had spoken to before.

"Not yet. Just an apprentice. But I know my potions."

"Really?" Finally, a bit of good luck. "Can you do a potion to make someone forget the last twenty-four hours?"

"Easy. I heard that pig Enwright send you away. I could do it for you for a thousand."

It sounded too good to be true. "Why would you do that? That other guy said there was no bartering."

"Because that other guy is the official guy. I'm more the under-the-table guy. How much of that four thousand do you think the actual mage gets paid? Most of it goes to the Chief, and greasers like Enwright. I can tell you none of it ends up in the apprentice's pockets." Blue's eyes glittered in the faint moonlight. "So you deal direct with me, I get a thousand bucks, you get your potion, and we're both happy. What do you say?"

"Are you sure you can do it?" What if this guy was just messing with him? Maybe he wasn't even a mage, just someone trying to squeeze a buck out of the situation. "What guarantee do I have your potion will work?"

The skinny goblin drew himself up to an unimpressive height. "I may only be an apprentice, but I know my shit. And what other choice do you have?"

He was right. There was no other choice. "Fine. When can you have it ready?"

"Give me an hour. Meet me back here. I'll wait for you outside the gate. Cash only."

An hour later Garth was back. Less than an hour, actually. He'd been to the ATM and gotten the cash, then he'd just wandered around killing time. He couldn't face going back to the apartment. Not until he had the potion.

He parked down the street and sat in the dark watching the gate. Nothing moved. Every few moments he checked his watch. When the hour was almost up a slight figure slipped out of the gate. Hunched over, it walked briskly down the street and stopped next to a bus shelter.

Garth shut his door quietly and moved across the street to the bus shelter.

"There you are," Blue said cheerily. "Got the money?"

Wordlessly Garth handed over the fold of notes. The goblin counted them carefully, then passed him a small pill bottle. Garth twisted off the lid and took a wary sniff of the clear liquid inside.

"How do I know this isn't just water?"

"You're a trusting soul, aren't you?"

"If this doesn't work …" Garth growled.

"Keep your shirt on. No need to be like that. There's enough for a couple of doses in there, in case you spill some." The goblin flapped his hands at him, shooing him away. "Off you go now. Don't want anyone seeing us here, do we? Oh, wait. Almost forgot." Blue fumbled another pill bottle, smaller than the first, out of his pocket and held it out. "You can add a couple of drops of this, if you like. It's just a sleeping potion. Sometimes it's easier that way. They wake up all fresh, can't remember a thing. Nastiness all gone."

"Thanks."

The goblin bared sharp teeth in a grin. "Pleasure doing business with you."

Garth drove home as fast as he could without getting a ticket. He took the stairs to the apartment two at a time, the precious potion clutched firmly in one big fist.

Trevor looked up as the door opened, relief blooming on his face. "Thank God."

"Where's Deb?"

"In the bedroom. Don't worry, I took her phone. She's just lying on the bed watching TV."

Garth tipped some of the potion into a small glass, then added a couple of drops of the sleeping potion, too. What the hell, it couldn't hurt. He took a deep breath, then opened the bedroom door.

"Hi, honey. How are you feeling?"

For answer, she scrambled across the bed to get away from him. "You can't keep me here forever, you know. People will notice if I don't go to work on Monday."

"No one's going to keep you here. Look, I brought you something to calm you down."

He held out the glass hopefully.

"I don't need calming down. I need you to get away from me. I never want to see you again."

She was off the bed now, pressed up against the wardrobe, staring at him as if he were her worst nightmare.

"Please, just drink this. You'll feel better."

"What is it?" She glared suspiciously at the glass. "Are you trying to turn me into a freak like you?"

She thought he was a freak. He drew another deep breath, trying to force a calm he didn't feel. "I'm not a freak, and I would never do anything to you that you didn't want. Just drink this, please."

He couldn't help the snarl that crept into the last words.

Her bottom lip quivered. "If I drink that, will you leave me alone?"

"I'll do anything you like. I'm not going to hurt you."

She reached across the bed for the glass. Her hand was trembling. He rounded the bed and pressed it into her hand, keeping his hand wrapped firmly around hers, though she shrank away from him. She might drop it, the way she was shaking, or change her mind and try to throw it away.

Together they brought the glass to her lips. Her eyes, huge with fear, watched him over the rim as she drank. She pulled a face, then shoved the empty glass back at him.

"Taste bad?"

"Horrible. What is it?"

Nothing dangerous, he hoped. He was putting a lot of trust in that scrawny goblin. This stuff better not hurt Deb in any way, or there'd be hell to pay.

"Just something to help you sleep."

"I'm not sleepy," she said immediately, but a massive yawn contradicted her. She sat down on the bed, her eyelids drooping.

"Why don't you have a rest? I'll wait outside. We can talk some more later."

She watched him as he backed toward the door, a reassuring smile plastered to his lips. She didn't move, as if reluctant to lie down when he was still so close. But as his hand closed on the door knob her eyes sagged shut and her head crashed onto the pillow. He flinched at the suddenness of it, and checked her pulse in a sudden rush of fear. It was strong and steady.

Quietly he left the room. Trevor hovered in the lounge room.

"Everything okay?"

Garth shrugged. "She's asleep. I guess we'll know when she wakes up." He flopped into an armchair and ran a weary hand over his eyes. "God, what a mess."

"But this'll fix it, right? She'll forget you ever told her?"

"So the goblin said. But there's still Janie."

"Who's Janie?"

"Friend of hers. Apparently she told her."

"She told her you're a werewolf? Shit. What are you going to do?"

Garth spoke without opening his eyes. Wrung out by the stress, he'd never felt so knackered. "I've got enough potion left. I just have to find a way to get it into her."

***

He was awake before Deb the next morning. In fact, he'd been awake half the night, sick with guilt. What if she never woke up? He didn't know what that goblin had put in the potion. He might have poisoned her, or messed with her brain. She might never be the same. Belatedly Garth had realised that a potion that altered someone's memory might have other, nastier side effects.

Why had he ever told her? Couldn't he have found some better way out of the argument than just blurting it out like that? He knew what was at stake; it wasn't something you could just go announcing to people as if you'd just changed jobs or bought a new car. This secret was deadly, and the only way to protect the people you cared for was to keep it from them forever.

He lay on the bed watching her. At last her eyelids fluttered, then she stretched luxuriously and yawned. Thank God.

"Hey there." She smiled at him. "How was your card night?"

He took a moment to answer her. He'd been thinking about this.

"The card night? That was the night before last. Don't you remember?"

The smile in her eyes faded, replaced by confusion. "The night before last? No, it was last night. Friday night. You were going straight to Trevor's from work."

He propped himself up on one elbow and arranged his face into an expression of loving concern. "Yes, that was Friday night. But last night was Saturday night. You had a bump on the head yesterday. The doctor said this might happen. Do you remember anything from Saturday?"

"A bump on the head?" Her hand crept up and felt around in her hair. "But I feel—I don't remember—"

"It's okay." He caught her questing hand and held it firmly. Her bewildered expression made him feel like the world's biggest jerk. "It's perfectly normal. It was just a little bump, but sometimes these things happen. Nothing to worry about."

"My head's not even sore. What happened?"

"You caught your foot on the rug. Tripped and banged your head on the corner of the coffee table. The doctor gave you some heavy-duty painkillers. Said you might feel a bit woozy today, and your memory might be screwy."

She slipped out of bed and peered at herself in the mirror on the dressing table, twisting this way and that to get a good look at herself. "If by screwy he meant completely gone … The last thing I remember is coming home from work on Friday night and getting ready to go to Janie's."

"Well, as long as you feel okay, that's the main thing."

She dragged the sleeve of her T-shirt up. "Well, I do have a bruise on this shoulder. And my back's a little sore. Otherwise I'm okay."

That was probably from when he'd knocked her flying in the lounge room as she ran sobbing for the door. Self-loathing rose like gorge in his throat.

"That's great." He turned away so he wouldn't have to watch her inspecting the bruises he'd put on her winter-pale skin, and hauled a T-shirt over his head. "How about we go out for breakfast, have a nice leisurely Sunday morning?"

"That sounds nice." She smiled at him in the mirror.

"You could invite Janie if you like."

He tried to keep his voice casual, but she still gave him a funny look. "Why? I didn't think you liked her that much."

"It's just that she left a few calls for you last night. She might be worried."

She came over and wrapped her arms around him. "That's so sweet. You're so thoughtful. I'll give her a ring and see what she's doing."

"Great."

He followed her out into the lounge room and tried not to look like he was listening in while she made the call.

"Yeah, I'm fine. Did you hear about my fall? Oh, nothing really, just a bit of amnesia … What?" She laughed, though it sounded a little forced. "No, of course not. I must have been joking. Do you want to meet us at Dorini's for breakfast? Yes, both of us. Okay then. Bye."

"She coming?"

"Yeah. Sounds like she's in a funny mood, though."

They walked to the café; it was only a couple of blocks away. The half-empty bottle rode snugly in the pocket of his jeans. Soon he'd find some opportunity to use it, and then life could go back to normal.

He held Deb's hand as they walked, and she smiled up at him.

"You're very quiet this morning. Are you okay?"

"I'm fine. Just didn't sleep very well."

"Were you worried about me?" He nodded, and she stretched up to kiss his cheek. "You're such a sweetie."

He smiled down at her, his thoughts far from sweet. The bottle in his pocket pressed against his hip with every stride, reminding him that last night she hadn't thought he was so sweet. *You're a freak! A monster!* Her eyes had been wide with terror and loathing. And she was right. He *was* a monster. He'd threatened her and frightened her, this woman he was supposed to love. He couldn't get the look on her face out of his mind.

The café was three-quarters full when they arrived. Seemed like everyone else had had the same idea: a bright sunny morning, a leisurely Sunday breakfast.

"You grab a table and I'll order some coffees," he said. "What will Janie have?"

"Get her a cappuccino. I'll have one, too."

It took a few moments to get to the counter and place the order. Deb snagged a table on the big veranda under a lopsided umbrella, and he weaved through the café toward her, table number in hand.

"It's a little chilly, but it's such a nice day it seemed a shame to sit inside," she said. "Though I wish they wouldn't let people bring their dogs."

There was a little yappy white thing two tables over, curled up at its owner's feet. Hardly bigger than a rat. Yet Deb still took the seat that put the table between her and it. He pulled out his phone and pretended to be checking messages while they waited. How could there be any future for someone like him with a woman who shrank from a puffball with pink bows in its hair?

Finally Deb spotted Janie standing in the doorway, and waved madly to attract her attention. Janie waved back, and started making her way through the crowded café. She got to their table just as the waitress arrived with three cappuccinos.

"Hi, darling, how are you?" Janie gave Deb her usual effusive greeting, complete with air kisses to both cheeks. While they were both occupied, Garth tipped the potion into one of the cups, then slid it over towards the spare seat. He'd taken the precaution of adding a couple of drops of Blue's sleeping potion to it beforehand: not as much as he'd given Deb last night, but hopefully enough to make Janie drowsy and a little confused. Otherwise it was going to be bloody difficult coming up with an explanation for why her memory suddenly went blank in the middle of breakfast. One woman with amnesia was weird enough; two would be ridiculously suspicious.

Janie pulled out the chair and sat down, giving him a look of mingled suspicion and dislike. She'd never taken to Garth, but that was okay, since the feeling was mutual. He found her unbearably plastic and fake; she thought he was a musclebound moron. And now, apparently, a cheating moron.

"Morning," she said. "Glad to see you're pretending to be human today."

"Hi." He ignored the sarcasm and took a big gulp of his coffee, and was pleased to see her do the same.

She put the cup back in the saucer and frowned at it. "God, it's bitter this morning. Pass the sugar."

Deb obliged, and Janie gave her a searching look. "Now tell me all about this accident of yours."

He could almost hear the air quotes around the word "accident". Clearly Janie wasn't buying the story.

"Oh, let's order first," Deb said. "I'm starving."

So they ordered, and while they were waiting for the food to arrive, Deb gave Janie the extended version of the accident he'd invented for her. Janie asked lots of questions, most of which Deb couldn't answer, so he was drawn into the conversation in spite of himself. Janie didn't mention his supposed infidelities, or make any more cracks about him being a werewolf. Clearly she was waiting until she could get Deb alone to give her the third degree about their relationship.

Finally the food came, which gave him the excuse to shovel bacon and sausage into his mouth and leave the talking to the women. By then they were on to less shaky ground: Janie was telling some long and apparently fascinating story about a girl they'd gone to school with. Garth watched her between bites, alert for any sign of the potion taking effect. But she chattered on as if everything were normal. Her breakfast was hardly touched, though he was pleased to see the coffee was nearly gone.

He eyed her bowl with revulsion. If his breakfast looked like that he probably wouldn't have eaten it either. It was a pile of some muesli drowned in yoghurt, and sprinkled with nuts and chunks of shrivelled fruit. Janie had stirred it all around until it looked like a bowl full of chunder. He concentrated on his own plate and prayed for the potion to work. Maybe it had to be taken fresh? The goblin hadn't said anything about that. But at least Janie wasn't looking at him like he was something she'd scraped off the bottom of her shoe any more. Maybe that was a good sign.

At long last the coffee was all drunk, and the muesli slop evidently pushed around the bowl enough. His own plate had been clean for a while when Janie looked at her watch and gave a little shriek.

"Oh, God, I'm late for work. What was I thinking, having breakfast on a Saturday?"

His heart leapt.

"It's not Saturday," Deb said.

Janie had been digging through her outsized handbag for her wallet. She looked up with a frown. "Of course it is. Annabelle will have had to open up without me. She'll be so cranky."

"No, it's not," Deb insisted, looking to him for confirmation. "It's Sunday. That's why we're here. You never do anything on a Saturday because of the shop."

Janie yawned. "I think I know what day of the week it is."

Garth reached behind him and snagged a Sunday paper off an empty table. He whacked it onto the tablecloth in front of Janie. Her face paled. It was a little hard to argue with a newspaper that had "Sunday" as part of its name.

"But …"

He felt a twinge of guilt at the look of panic on her face. Just a twinge, mind you. Janie was far from being his favourite person. Still, it was a cruel thing to mess with her mind. Cruel but necessary, unfortunately. She yawned again while they both stared at her.

"You've been working too hard, that's the trouble." Deb laid a comforting hand on her friend's arm. "No wonder you're all mixed up—look at you! You can hardly keep your eyes open. Just as well it *is* Sunday, you can go home and rest."

"I can't believe it." Janie shook her head, muttering to herself. "What did I do yesterday?"

"Went to work, of course. What else would you do on a Saturday?" Deb grinned, trying to make light of the situation. "Come on, I'm the one with amnesia!"

Janie made an effort to smile, though she was clearly still troubled by her confusion. "You're right. I must be more tired than I thought. How weird."

"Go home and rest. You look exhausted. Doesn't she, Garth?"

"Very tired," he said, as another enormous yawn practically unhinged her jaw. "You look like you're out on your feet." She waved her wallet vaguely in his direction and he held up a hand to forestall her. "Don't worry about that. I'll pay. You just head home and get yourself to bed. You didn't drive, did you?"

That would be all he needed, for her to crash her car on the way home.

"No, I walked."

She got to her feet, swaying a little, and Deb stood up, too, to kiss her goodbye. He watched them hugging, two women with holes in their memories, and felt sick. This was what his life would be like forever now, full of secrets and lies. He'd shown Deb his real self, and she'd rejected him. He'd been a fool to expect anything else. The woman was frightened of dogs, for God's sake, even little yappy things. A full-grown werewolf was no lap dog. How could he have imagined her reaction might have been any different?

And knowing that, how could he stay? Did he really want to live like that, hiding an integral part of his identity from his partner? Always sneaking around, making up an excuse every month to get away, putting up with her growing suspicions. She'd followed him this time, sure he was cheating on her just because of some comment Janie had made. It wouldn't be long before it occurred to her again, and then where would he be?

Now he understood why wolves usually partnered within the pack. He got to his feet, a fake smile on his face, and said goodbye to Janie. His heart was heavy with the knowledge that soon he'd have to say goodbye to Deb as well.

SIXTY-SIXTH MOON
Five years a werewolf

He'd left the car far behind and hiked into the national park. It was a weekend, which meant there might be people out camping, but he was a long way from any camp grounds. He'd made sure to pick a lonely spot. Weeknights were better, but he had no control over the timing of the full moon.

The weather wasn't too great for camping either. If he'd had any choice, he'd have been home, warm and dry, not out here in the cold, dank bush. It wasn't raining now, but it had bucketed down just after he'd left the car. Wet clothes hadn't improved his mood any. He was looking forward to getting his gear off. The wolf wouldn't mind the wet.

His boots made no noise on the soggy ground as he walked. The air was cool and filled with the smells of moist earth, rotting bark, eucalyptus, even a hint of lemon from a lemon-scented gum. His wolf nose would be able to pick out a lot more. He saw the occasional track in muddy patches of ground: there would be roos out here, maybe deer or pigs. Definitely smaller game, like rabbits and possums. The bush would come alive at night, and his wolf would be ready.

Tonight would mark the first anniversary of living as a lone wolf. He'd had a gutful of Rhys and his mates, and the beta, Sean, always niggling at him, trying to prove their dominance. He'd shut Rhys's buddy Jensen up by battling him into submission, but that had only made Rhys even more determined to bring him to heel. And who had time for that shit? He just wanted to be left alone, not dragged into their stupid pack politics.

He didn't care any more who Carly chose to spend her life with, but that didn't mean he wanted to spend every full moon watching Rhys flaunt his relationship with her. He might have been able to take Rhys in a fight, but the whole pack thing made him sick. He hated the way his instincts pushed him to cower every time the alpha walked past. He and Kevin had never seen eye to eye, and he hadn't bowed to him as a boy. It nearly killed him to submit to him as a grown man.

His mother had been right. He wasn't a natural fit as a wolf. He'd been the outsider all his life; he didn't even know *how* to fit in any more. And yet that was what pack life was all about: fitting in, knowing your place. What did you do when you had no place?

Well, you left. That had been his answer, after four years of never quite making pack life work. He didn't need that kind of stress in his life. Kevin would never have let him go, so he hadn't given Kevin a bloody option, just moved to a smaller town without telling anyone. He'd been living as a lone wolf for a year now, and he couldn't see what all the fuss was about. He still felt the pull of the pack bond, that yearning to be part of something bigger than himself, but he'd learned to ignore it. Out here on his own, he answered to no one, and that was just how he liked it.

When he felt the moon stirring in his blood he stripped off and stuffed his clothes in his backpack. Goosebumps prickled on his bare skin as he turned to face east, where the moon would appear. Leaf litter squelched beneath his feet, and drips from the trees overhead worked their chilly way down his spine as he waited.

The change caught him in its painful grip, broke his bones, tore at his innards. He writhed on the ground, kicking up the damp leaves and leaving deep grooves scored in the detritus. The agony was mercifully brief; it seemed the longer he'd been a wolf the faster the change became. It was never as bad as that first soul-destroying time, when he'd seriously felt he'd rather die than have to go through that every month.

The wolf rose to its feet and shook briskly from nose to tail, sending water and bits of leaf and twig flying. A smorgasbord of smells greeted him, and he sniffed appreciatively. Rain had blurred the specifics, but the heavy scent of tusker pervaded the area. That would make a meal to blunt even his great appetite.

He set off in a jaunty trot, following the stories his nose told him. It was dark here under the trees. The moon had barely peeked above the horizon, and she wouldn't light the way until she'd climbed higher in the sky, but his night vision was good, even better than a natural wolf's. He surprised a rabbit, but that barely made a snack. He had his heart set now on pig.

Despite the pervasiveness of their scent, pigs proved hard to find. His long legs had eaten up a lot of ground, and the moon was well up, before the scent intensified enough to warn him one was near. He stopped in darker shadows at the base of a towering gum and sniffed the air.

Young saplings dotted the immediate area, their leaves whispering secrets as they stirred in a slight breeze. Bracken filled in the space around their knees, green and lush. The breeze wafted the scent of pig to his nose and as he stood quietly the bracken waved as something large moved through it. He caught flashes of a dappled body, and a quiet grunting as it rooted around in the undergrowth.

Since he was downwind, it had no idea he was here, and he gathered himself to attack, saliva spurting into his mouth already. And then the pig stuck its hoary head out of the ferns, looking around suspiciously. The tusks on it were massive. As they caught the light he felt a rush of memory: his first hunt, and the feeling of tusks like that ripping their way down his flank.

He held still, trembling with the effort of resisting the urge to leap at it. More of the pig emerged from the bracken, and then more still. The thing was huge, longer than him and twice as heavy. A pack could have surrounded it, harried it. Bled it and brought it down. But he had no pack. There was only him.

His blood was up, but he was no longer the impatient cub he had been. Those tusks probably couldn't kill him, but they could leave him to spend the night on the ground, lost in a healing coma. And then there would be no fresh meat spurting blood into his mouth. The moon drove him to the hunt, and he would have to kill soon, but he had just enough control to choose a better target. Where there was one pig, there would be others. He let the pig wander off, oblivious to how close it had come to death.

He ranged through the night, hearing the skitterings as smaller prey scurried to safety, watching for another pig-sized shivering in the undergrowth. Another deeper rumbling noise teased at him, too, but he ignored it, focused on his quarry. He would have to kill soon. The urge was becoming overwhelming. At last his nose caught the scent again, and he startled another, much smaller than the first giant tusker.

He must have made a noise at the last minute, because it looked up as he leapt. With a squeal, it dodged around a group of saplings and shot off into the trees. He gave chase, swift and deadly, shouldering through bushes and leaping over rocks.

The pig was barely half his size, and nimble. Its desperate swerves and dodges saved its life a number of times, but the undergrowth started to thin out, leaving it with nowhere to hide. The wolf put on a burst of speed and was almost on it when it suddenly burst out of the trees into a field full of stubble. Rows of some crop had been harvested, and the remains were just high enough to hide a pig.

Now the rumbling noise was louder, and lights swung crazily in the distance, but the wolf focused on the pig as it darted in and out of the stubble. His claws raked its back and it squealed, the sound carrying across the moonlit field, but it managed to evade him yet again.

A spotlight swept across them, and the rumbling resolved into the roar of a diesel engine. The spotlight swung wildly as the truck it was mounted on bounced across the uneven ground. A gun barked, but the wolf ignored it. The pig, however, swerved away from the lights and noise, and plunged back into the relative safety of the bush.

The gun cracked again. The pig squealed, hit, and the wolf leapt, his jaws closing on its shoulder. They both went down, crashing through the underbrush. The wolf sank his teeth into the pig's throat, and hot salty blood spurted as he ripped it out. He tore at the steaming flesh, swallowing great chunks in his frenzy.

The glare of a spotlight found him, half-hidden among the bushes, and he growled, his great head swinging toward the light. Who came to disturb his kill? He stood over it protectively.

"What the hell is that?" said a man's voice.

"Jesus. That's the biggest wild dog I've ever seen," said another. The spotlight quivered in his hand.

"Shoot the bastard. He's got our pig."

The wolf growled, all the hackles on his shoulders standing up.

"You want to eat it after he's ripped into it? Holy shit, look at its eyes! They're glowing."

"It's just the light. Don't be such a pussy. You afraid of a little doggy?"

"That's no doggy, that's a friggin monster."

"Then we'd better not leave it running around out here, hey?"

A shot rang out. The wolf took a step forward, its growls rising to a thunderous pitch.

"You missed!"

"Did not. Jesus." The man unloaded the rifle into the wolf, but it made no difference. The wolf leapt at his attacker. The man turned to run, but was knocked to the ground, the wolf's claws on his back, its jaws at his throat.

Early morning sun slanting through the trees and into his eyes woke Garth. The wolf had found his way back to his clothes in the night. It was a brisk spring morning, so he rose and put them on before anything dropped off from the cold, discovering two round, puckered scars on his aching shoulder that hadn't been there before. It was sprinkling again, and looked like turning into a determined drizzle, so he shouldered his backpack gingerly and set off for the car. Maybe he could reach it before he got completely soaked.

He wasn't hungry. The wolf must have fed well last night. Where had those scars come from? He remembered chasing a pig, tree trunks and bushes flashing past in a wild blur, then the thrill as his teeth closed on its throat. How human it had sounded as it screamed.

Wait.

Garth stopped, mouth suddenly dry. He hadn't … A chill that had nothing to do with the weather stole over him. No, he couldn't have. That was why he'd come all the way out here, to the middle of nowhere. Far from any humans.

But … he remembered a field. A cultivated field. How far had the wolf ranged last night in search of pig? He leaned against a tree trunk, sick with foreboding. Flashes of memory assaulted him: a spotlight dazzling in the night, the sound of gunfire. *That's the biggest wild dog I've ever seen.*

Oh, no. No, no, no. He sagged against the tree, his stomach churning. The scream, so abruptly cut off, the hot gush of blood coursing down his throat.

He bent over and heaved his guts up onto the wet ground. Hot tears threatened, and he squeezed his eyes tight shut. *This* was why a wolf needed a pack. An alpha would never let his pack attack a human being, and an alpha was the only thing that could rein in his wolf when the full moon called to him.

He wiped his mouth and leaned his tear-streaked face against the rough bark of the gum tree. He'd killed a man. Worse, he'd killed a man *and eaten his flesh.* He gagged at the very thought, but there was nothing left in his stomach to bring up. Deb had been right. He was a monster.

ONE HUNDRED AND NINETY-SECOND MOON
Fifteen years a werewolf

Jerry glanced at him as they drove out of the motel carpark.

"Do I look okay?"

She was wearing what he thought of as her usual uniform: black jeans, Doc Martens, and a black T-shirt. The T-shirt was plain, which was a thoughtful gesture. Most of the ones she owned were either plastered with skulls or swear words.

"Relax, would you? It's just a barbecue. No big deal." He wore T-shirt and jeans himself, though his T-shirt had *Trust me, I'm a Jedi* printed on it.

"Yeah, but it's your dad's seventieth birthday party, and I've never met him before."

"You'll be fine." He'd given up telling people that Kevin wasn't his dad. Maybe he'd finally mellowed a bit. Or maybe it was just that he didn't have to live with him any more. He'd spent the past ten years in Melbourne as part of the Melbourne pack. After realising that he couldn't live as a lone wolf, pack life seemed the only option, but he'd had enough of the Sydney pack. Trevor had suggested a change of scenery, and so he'd headed south, and been there ever since.

He grinned at Jerry. "Besides, who's going to notice what you're wearing with that hair?"

She touched her hair, spiked and died a violent purple, and grinned back. "I reckon purple's my colour."

"I don't know, I liked the blue myself."

"A girl needs a change now and then."

"True. You been to Sydney before?"

"A couple of times. Only in the city, though. Been to the zoo, climbed the Harbour Bridge. You know, the touristy stuff. Never been out here in the suburbs."

They'd checked into a motel a few minutes' drive from the pack house, despite his mother's insistence that he should stay over. Probably half the pack would be crashing there tonight, and he just wasn't interested. He'd go to the party, because if he missed it it would break her heart, but he was out of there as soon as it was socially acceptable to leave. There'd be no sitting round the campfire singing kumbaya with his old packmates.

He turned into a street lined with huge old oak trees. This was all familiar territory.

"It's pretty," Jerry said. "Leafy."

"Yeah."

"Thanks for bringing me."

He glanced across at her. She was only a kid, twenty-four years old. At least, now that he was thirty-seven, that felt like a kid to him. She'd managed to fit a fair bit of living into those twenty-four years. Being gay in a werewolf pack was almost as bad as being moonborn. Werewolves, with the odd exception, tended to be macho arseholes, and Jerry had had a lot to put up with. The Melbourne pack wasn't her birth pack either. She'd moved around a lot, seeking an acceptance that was proving pretty damn elusive.

"Seemed like you needed a break. Besides, you're doing me a favour. If I turned up alone, Mum would only nag me about why I haven't settled down with some nice werewolf girl. With you there she'll have to be polite."

"Why haven't you?" She put her booted feet up on the dashboard, perfectly at ease in his company. "The ladies should be knocking each other down in the rush. I mean, guys aren't really my thing, but you're pretty hot. And you're not as much of a shithead as most werewolves."

"Gee, thanks."

She ignored his sarcasm. "I bet Amy would go out with you if you asked her. She'd jump at the chance."

That was because Amy was so submissive she'd do anything someone above her in the pack hierarchy asked. But he didn't want a woman who was little more than a slave; he wanted a partner. Someone who would call him out on his bullshit. Someone who liked him for *him*, not just because of his status—or lack of it. The galling fact was that dominant she-wolves looked down on moonborn just as much as the males did. His only chance was to find another moonborn female, or take a submissive partner. Moonborn females were pretty thin on the ground, and the other option turned his stomach.

"I'm not interested in Amy." He hadn't had a serious relationship since he'd broken up with Deb all those years ago. Humans were *definitely* out of the equation. He'd learned his lesson.

"Well, you're going to get old and bitter. Old*er*, anyway."

"Right, you're giving relationship advice now. Because your love life is so damned good."

She laughed. "Nobody wants us. We'll just have to end up two lonely old broken-down werewolves together."

"Only if you dye your hair back to blue."

"Anything for you, darling."

He pulled up across the street from the pack house.

"This is nice," she said.

Perched above the street, the house blended into the gum trees that surrounded it. Wooden stairs climbed from street level up to a spacious deck built onto the front, lit by the soft glow of lanterns. All the action was obviously happening around the back, judging by the music and laughter drifting from the rear of the property.

"It's not bad." Not big enough for the Sydney pack, but not bad now that he didn't have to live here.

"I can't believe Kevin's seventy. It seems so old for an alpha."

"That's just because you're used to our pack." Avery, the Melbourne alpha, was thirty-five, two years younger than Garth himself. "There's no reason a seventy-year-old can't be an alpha."

Wolves weren't like people. Their lifespan was the same as humans', but they didn't spend their twilight years in a steady decline. All those years of violent metamorphosis took a silent toll, until one day their shifter ability to heal suddenly failed them. If they didn't die in pack squabbles, they dropped dead of a heart attack in their eighties or nineties, still as outwardly fit as when they were fifty.

He got out of the car and looked across the road, dreading going in there again. Despite his words to Jerry, he was worried. Seventy was old to be a pack leader, not because the alpha was no longer up to the job, but because by that time there were usually younger wolves eyeing off the top spot. Kevin might be as fit as a fifty-year-old but that still wasn't the same as the fitness of a man in his thirties or forties. Kevin had been lucky that the younger wolves in the pack were too lazy to want the responsibilities that came with being an alpha. Rhys was in his early forties now, the prime of life for a werewolf. If he'd had any kind of ambition, Kevin would have faced a challenge by now. He was lucky that Rhys's father, Sean, was a loyal beta. Garth couldn't stand the man, but he couldn't fault his loyalty. Plenty of alphas had been toppled by their betas.

He worried about what would happen to Mum if Kevin wasn't around. All her status came from him. She was only moonborn, and he knew perfectly well how they were treated. It would all depend on who became leader after Kevin.

Best not to think about such things, particularly on the man's seventieth birthday. They were supposed to be celebrating his achievements, not wondering how much longer he'd last. *Many happy returns, Kev.* He hoped his stepfather lived to a hundred.

A familiar figure appeared on the deck. Trevor had filled out since the last time Garth had seen him, on a flying visit to Melbourne.

"You been working out, bro?" he called. "Didn't think accountants had time for that."

"Get stuffed." Trevor grinned and gave him a quick, hard hug as he reached the top of the stairs. "It's good to see you."

Garth introduced Jerry, and then a young woman joined them, and his mouth just about fell open.

"Mac? Is that you?"

"Hi, Garth!" She gave him a hug, too.

"I hardly recognised you!"

"If you tell me how much I've grown, I'll punch you. It's been ten years, Garth. You should have visited."

She tossed her dark hair over her shoulder, her huge blue eyes giving him a challenging stare. She was a stunner. She'd always been a pretty child, but now that prettiness had blossomed into the fresh beauty of a woman on the verge of life. She wore no makeup, but she didn't need it. Her skin was perfect, her eyes divine. She wore nothing but a bikini, and she'd grown some curves since last time he saw her, too.

He turned to introduce Jerry, and saw she was just as stunned as he was, though maybe not for the same reason. Mac was way too young for him, and he thought of her as a kid sister besides, but Jerry was clearly smitten.

"I even invited you to my twenty-first, but you didn't come."

"Sorry. But I'm here now. This is my packmate, Jerry."

"Hi, Jerry." Mac stuck out her hand and Jerry took it in both of hers.

"Hi. I'm feeling kind of overdressed for this party now."

Mac laughed. "I can lend you something if you want to swim. You look about the same size as me."

She tucked her arm through Jerry's and led them inside. She and Jerry disappeared toward one of the bedrooms while Trevor took Garth out to the entertaining area out back. A big banner proclaimed "Happy 70th birthday, Kevin!" in cheerful red letters. That would be Mum's doing. A goat was roasting on a spit, and half a dozen men were gathered around a keg. That would be Kevin's.

Mum saw him and her face lit up. She looked as good as ever, not a single grey hair on her head. Obviously Garth took after his father since his temples were already silvering.

"It's so good to see you!" She crushed him in a hug that lasted just a little longer than it should have, and there was a suspicious brightness in her eyes when she released him. He'd kept in touch by phone and Skype, and she'd been down to Melbourne a few times, but now he felt slack for not coming back to Sydney before now. Mac was right. Ten years was a long time. "Come in! Everyone's here."

She took him by the arm and drew him over toward the table where the alpha and his most senior wolves were seated. Some of the guests had been here quite a while, if the noise level was any indication, and had been fairly dedicated to the consumption of alcohol in that time. He saw Rhys and a couple of his friends in the pool, floating around in inflatable rings, beers in hand. Rhys lifted his glass in sardonic salute. Garth gave him a brief nod. Arsehole.

Kevin rose to greet him, which was quite a compliment. Maybe the old bastard was pleased to see him, too. Or maybe he wasn't such a bastard after all. With the benefit of maturity, Garth could admit that maybe he hadn't been the easiest stepson.

Kevin clasped him in a firm hug. "Good to have you back. You should visit more often."

"Yeah." Not likely. His life was in Melbourne now. Just being here made him feel like that angry young guy again, trying and failing to fit in. It wasn't a pleasant feeling.

"Your mother misses you, you know."

"Lucky she's got Trev, then." His brother handed him a beer and he took a long grateful swallow. "Thanks, mate. A man could die of thirst in this heat."

He exchanged some stilted conversation about the weather with his stepfather, all the while sizing up his old pack. Sean gave him a mocking wave. The beta was a little greyer, but largely unchanged, still thin as a whipcord. The younger wolves in the pool ignored him.

Carly was also in the pool, her skin a golden brown, her body as lithe and lovely as Garth remembered. She looked good enough to eat—but he was pleased to find he'd lost his appetite for that particular dish. Maybe he was a slow learner, but her steadfast rejection of him had sunk in eventually.

Rhys heaved himself out of the water in one fluid motion and began towelling himself dry. His body was well-muscled, as powerful as ever. Carly climbed out after him and wrapped a sarong around her glistening body.

"Get me another beer, babe," Rhys said, stretching out on a lounger by the pool.

Useless git. He had hands, didn't he? Why didn't he get his own bloody beer? Being treated like a servant didn't seem to bother Carly, though. She turned away without comment and filled a glass at the keg.

Jerry came out with Mac, wearing considerably fewer clothes than she'd had on when they'd arrived. Mac had found her a pink bikini splashed with purple flowers which almost matched her spiky hair. A few eyebrows rose at the sight of her and Garth hurried over.

"Mum, this is my friend Jerry. We're packmates."

He could see the calculation in his mother's eyes as she jumped to all the wrong conclusions.

"Lovely to meet you, Jerry," she said. "Thank you for coming."

"My pleasure." Jerry flashed him a grin; she knew exactly what his mother was thinking.

She followed Mac to the pool and they dived in. Several sets of eyes followed, too, Rhys's among them. So when Carly thrust the glass of beer into his hand he fumbled it and beer went everywhere, the glass smashing at his feet.

"Stupid bitch!" He leapt up, dripping beer, and cuffed her on the side of the head.

Garth closed the distance between them in two strides and shoved the bastard hard. Rhys's heel caught on the edge of the pool, and he fell in. When he spluttered to the surface there was murder in his eyes. He hauled himself out with a snarl.

"That's enough, boys!" Kevin said sharply.

Rhys didn't even look at him. His father appeared at his side and took a firm grip on his shoulders.

"Rhys." Sean's voice held a warning note.

"It's a party, Garth," his mother chided. "Let's not have any fighting."

Garth folded his arms across his chest. "Tell that to the caveman here. He's the one beating up on his girlfriend."

Rhys tried to shake his father off, but Sean held firm. "Enough. You've had too much to drink."

Oh, *now* Sean tried to rein in his son? Why hadn't he ever bothered when Rhys was younger and it might have done some good? Not much point starting now.

Rhys growled, but Garth just stared, impassive. The days when Rhys could whip him with one hand tied behind his back were a long time ago. Let him try. He might find that they were gone forever.

"Why do you put up with this crap?" he asked Kevin, without taking his eyes off Rhys. What the hell, this wasn't his pack any more. He had nothing to lose by putting his stepfather on the spot. "He's been throwing his weight around ever since I can remember, picking fights, causing trouble."

He was so sick of the bullying that was as much a part of werewolf culture as howling at the moon. You were gay, or you were moonborn, or maybe you were just lower down the pecking order. Some wolves didn't even need a reason. But he didn't remember it being quite this bad. Rhys had never attacked his own mate in the days when Garth had been part of the pack. Maybe Kevin was already too old to be the alpha. Seemed like he was losing control.

Rhys strained against his father's grip. "You think you can take me, you moonborn piece of shit?"

"I think I can chew you up and spit you out." He clenched his fists, feeling the rush of adrenaline. His wolf wanted out, wanted to rip and tear, but he wrestled it under control. He wanted to do this man to man so he could truly appreciate the look in Rhys's eyes when the moonborn piece of shit hammered him into the ground.

"Stand down!" Kevin barked, but Rhys was too drunk to respond to the signals his wolf would be frantically sending at that tone in his alpha's voice. If Kevin wanted obedience, he would have to get it the hard way.

Garth's wolf bristled. He didn't have to listen any more, since Kevin wasn't his alpha.

"If you won't do your job, I'll do it for you," he snarled at his stepfather. "Someone should have dealt with this arsehole years ago."

Rhys tore out of his father's hands and hurled himself forward, his right arm swinging in a punch that would have taken Garth's head off if it had connected. Garth sidestepped and slammed his own fist into Rhys's ear as he staggered past. Onlookers moved hastily out of the way, forming a concerned circle around them. Kevin made a grab for Rhys, but the younger wolf shrugged him off and came roaring back toward Garth, his red face twisted in rage.

This time his fist glanced off Garth's shoulder. There was power in that blow, despite his drunkenness. Garth countered with a blow to Rhys's solar plexus that doubled him over, then brought his knee up into his face while he was down there. The crunch of Rhys's nose breaking was like music to his ears.

Roughly he wrestled the other man to the ground and pressed his bleeding face to the paving. He dropped his knee into Rhys's back, and twisted his right arm up behind him.

He leaned close and spoke into Rhys's ear. "Tell Carly you're sorry."

Rhys spat blood. "Fuck you."

Garth applied more pressure to the arm. "Tell Carly you're sorry, or I'll break your friggin arm off and stuff it down your throat."

Seconds ticked past in tense silence.

"Sorry," Rhys grunted.

"I don't think she heard you." Garth twisted harder.

"I'm sorry," Rhys gasped. Sweat mingled with the blood dribbling down his face. He looked bad and stank worse, but Garth didn't give a crap.

"For what?"

"For—Jesus! For hitting you."

"Let him go, Garth." Carly stood over them. "He said he was sorry."

"And for calling her a bitch," Garth prompted. One more twist and the arm really would break. It couldn't happen to a nicer guy.

"And for—for calling you a bitch."

Rhys whimpered in relief as Garth released him and stepped back. Carly bent down to help him up. Her voice murmured sympathy, but her eyes were on Garth, and there was a speculative gleam in them that he'd never seen before.

***

Garth checked his watch. The candles had been blown out and the cake had been cut, and now he and Trevor were sitting in the shadows on the far side of the pool. Surely soon he could excuse himself and get out of here. Rhys and his cronies had been staring daggers at him all night. Carly had been giving him a look that was even more alarming. No one was as relaxed as they were trying to appear. Kevin's party would certainly be remembered, but probably not for the right reasons. When he considered all the trouble his mother had gone to, that made him feel guilty, and guilt gave him indigestion.

Or maybe that was the cake. He pushed a mountain of cream around his plate with his fork, trying to make it look as though he'd eaten more than he really had. Mum had always had such a sweet tooth.

There was another peal of laughter from the corner where Mac and Jerry were holed up together like best friends who hadn't seen each other in years. They were getting on like a house on fire. At least someone was enjoying the party. It didn't look as though the birthday boy was having a great time, despite Mum's efforts. Guilt gnawed at him again at the tense expression on his stepfather's face.

"Kev looks like he's swallowed a lemon," he said to Trevor.

His brother gave him an impatient look. "You're an idiot."

"Why?"

"You've undermined him. Of course he's pissed. You've made him look weak in front of his own pack."

"But he wasn't doing anything!" Sean glanced their way and he made an effort to lower his voice. "Are we just supposed to sit back and let that jerk throw his weight around?"

"If Carly didn't object and the pack leader didn't object, it's not your place to ride in on your white horse. When are you going to learn to think before you act? Everything you do has consequences—not just for you but for others. That's what being part of a pack is about. We're all connected."

He wasn't used to being lectured by his little brother. Sometimes he forgot that Trevor was a grown man now. A sensible one, too, who'd never had any trouble finding his place in life, the lucky bastard.

"Well, thank God I'm not connected to this lot any more. This isn't the way they do things in Melbourne, let me tell you. Avery would never stand for Rhys's behaviour."

Or mine, probably. Avery certainly didn't take kindly to challenges to his authority as the alpha, though he usually turned a blind eye to the verbal bullying that went on. Hence Jerry's desire to come with Garth tonight. He watched her throw back her purple head and laugh at something that Mac had just whispered to her. He hadn't seen her look that happy in ages.

Trevor took another swig of his beer and said nothing.

A pair of golden legs appeared beside them.

"Mind if I join you?"

He looked up and found Carly smiling down at him. It was a free country. He shrugged and she dragged a chair over next to his.

"I wanted to thank you for … before."

Trevor gave him a warning look. Okay, he'd got the message. The less said about the whole thing the better.

"No problem."

"I haven't seen you for so long!" she continued brightly. "Tell me what you've been up to."

Well, that could make a long and ugly story. He gave her a condensed version, mainly focusing on life with the Melbourne pack and his job there. Being a nightclub bouncer wasn't as glamorous as it sounded, but it paid well and supplied him with plenty of amusing stories for conversations like this one.

Carly laughed in all the right places, leaning toward him to catch every word. He could almost forget all the intervening years as she smiled and twirled her hair thoughtfully around one finger, as if he was that lovestruck boy again.

Almost.

But he wasn't a boy, and Carly was just a woman. Still a pretty woman, but he didn't long for her as if she were the sun his world revolved around any more. It was nice to chat, like any two grown people, but that was as far as it went. His wolf no longer pined for hers.

Rhys appeared out of the dark and Garth's wolf, which had basically been napping through the conversation, sat up and took notice. His rivalry with Rhys went way beyond their competition over Carly. Having to spend time with him set his teeth on edge.

"Come inside, Carls," Rhys said.

"In a minute," she said. "I'm just chatting with the boys."

Rhys turned his red-rimmed eyes on Garth and a beast looked out of them. The hairs on the back of Garth's neck prickled, but he didn't move from his relaxed position.

"You better watch yourself around my girl."

"Or what?" Out of the corner of his eye he saw Trevor shaking his head at him, but he couldn't ignore a direct challenge. "You want me to break your arm for real next time?"

Rhys's face twisted into a snarl, and Garth tensed, expecting the other man to launch himself at him. Trevor gripped the arms of his chair, ready to leap into action if necessary, but after a moment's silent glaring, Rhys spun on his heel and headed into the house.

Trevor blew out a long frustrated breath. "Maybe you should go. He's only going to get drunker. If you can't stop baiting him, this isn't going to end well."

"He challenged me. What do you expect me to do?"

"I expect you to remember it's Dad's birthday and try and keep your wolf under control. It's one night, Garth. Is that so much to ask?"

"Fine. I'll go then." Aware that he sounded like a sulky child, he made an effort to smile at Carly as he stood. "It's been lovely catching up with you."

She rose, too, and zoomed in for a kiss that lingered just a fraction too long. She looked up at him through sultry eyelashes. "The pleasure's been all mine."

He smiled, his heart speeding up a little in spite of himself, and went to find Mum. Trevor was right; it was time to go.

Mum was in the kitchen, fussing with the washing up. As the pack alpha, she could have palmed that job off onto one of the juniors, but she liked to keep busy.

"I'm going to head off, Mum." He put his arms around her still-trim waist from behind and gave her a hug. "It's been a great party."

She dropped the dishcloth in the sink and shook suds off her hands. "So soon? Are you coming to lunch tomorrow?"

Turning in the circle of his arms, she tipped her head up to look at him. She only came up to his shoulder. Not that that made any difference, of course. She still bossed him around as if he were three years old.

"Nah. I've got a long drive to get back to Melbourne. I have to work on Monday."

The hopeful light in her eyes dimmed and he felt like a jerk. Still, after tonight's effort, he was probably better off staying away. Rhys just brought out the worst in him.

"Oh, dear," she said. "And I hardly got a chance to speak to your friend Jerry. She seems nice."

He grinned. "Mac seems to think so."

One hand stroked his shoulder, smoothing out an imagined crease in his shirt. "I wish you came home more often, Garth. I hardly ever see you any more."

He held out his hands helplessly. "Sorry, but you know how it is. Work's so busy."

"Yes, I know how it is." He could tell from the sadness in her eyes that she wasn't talking about his work. Then she slapped him smartly on the chest. "Still, you could do a better job of keeping in touch. Would it kill you to ring your mother occasionally?"

Then her gaze darted to the side and she said in a very different tone: "What are you doing with that?"

Garth spun around and saw Rhys in the doorway. He held a knife—a knife that Garth had only seen once before, under the light of a full moon, but he'd never forgotten it. The blade gleamed dimly in the harsh kitchen lights. What the hell was Rhys doing with it? That knife should be locked away. It buzzed with wrongness, its very being a threat to everyone in this house. That knife could have taken his life, all those years ago on a boulder-strewn hill somewhere in the Blue Mountains. If he hadn't risen from his first change sane and whole, Kevin would have ended him with a simple swipe of its deadly silver blade.

Garth's eyes flicked up towards Rhys's face. The whites of Rhys's eyes were bloodshot with alcohol, but his irises were pure yellow, the sign that his wolf was very close to the surface. Though he wore the shape of a man, there was very little humanity left in him. It was drowned in bloodlust and drink, washed away as the wolf howled for vengeance.

Garth shoved his mother behind him as Rhys advanced, the knife thrust out before him.

"Put that down this instant," Mum snapped, "or you will be banished from this pack."

"Maybe I don't want to be in this pack any more. Filthy moonborn. Should kill you both."

The knife tip wavered in the air, then slashed toward them. Garth dodged away, pushing his mother toward the back door.

"Get out, Mum. I'll handle him."

His mother slipped outside, calling for Kevin, her voice shrill with panic. Garth breathed out a sigh of relief that she was gone, out of the danger zone. Now he could focus on disarming Rhys without worrying about her. There was no room for error here. One scratch was all it would take to end him.

"Put the knife down, Rhys. You don't want to do this."

Rhys feinted again, another wild swing of the blade. Garth leapt out of the way, heart thundering.

"Don't I?" Rhys's voice was harsh, almost a growl. "Should have done this years ago. Pity I didn't know the combination of his safe back then."

He'd stolen it from Kevin's safe? He'd be lucky if Kevin didn't kill him.

Garth leapt forward as Rhys lunged again, and caught his wrist in a grip of iron. Behind him, a burst of sound as half a dozen people rushed into the room. But he didn't even look; he was too focused on the struggle for the blade that wavered between their two bodies.

Someone shoulder-charged him, knocking him aside. He saw a hand reaching out, the blade flicking toward it. A line of bright blood appeared, and someone screamed, a high-pitched wail that momentarily stilled the room.

He stared, not understanding what he was seeing. Kevin was on his knees, clutching at his hand as blood dripped to the floor. He grunted, an animal sound of pain that formed a counterpoint to Garth's mother's desperate, hysterical shrieks. Everyone was shouting at once. People were running, crying, falling to the floor beside Kevin, whose hand was swelling before their eyes. Already it was twice its normal size. Ominous black lines spread like crazed spider webs under Kevin's swollen skin, coursing up his arm as he threw back his head and howled in agony. The sound pierced Garth's heart with slivers of ice. Sick with dread, he met Kevin's pain-filled eyes and had to turn away from the despair he saw there.

Kevin had been cut by silver. Kevin was a dead man.

Now he was on the floor, writhing as the poison spread through his blood. He screamed himself hoarse, Mum sobbing at his side, trying to comfort him. His face was so contorted and swollen it looked as if his head might burst like an overinflated balloon if someone put a pin to it. Someone in the crowd murmured *oh my God oh my God* over and over again, but not even God could fix this. Mum tried to cradle him in her lap, but his agonized convulsions jerked him out of her reaching hands. As his eyes glazed over, it seemed doubtful he could still understand her desperate sobbed endearments.

Through it all, Rhys stood with the deadly blade held loosely at his side. Had everyone forgotten him? Shuddering, Garth dragged his eyes away from the hideous scene on the floor, murder in his heart. He had not forgotten.

He closed with Rhys, one arm snaking around his neck from behind, the other reaching for the knife. Melbourne had given him quite an education in the use of knives, and Rhys was holding it like an amateur.

"Stop!" Sean cried.

Garth seized the knife and plunged it into Rhys's neck. Now he would stop. He stood back and watched dispassionately as the black lines spread their creeping death and the screaming started all over again.

***

"Give me the knife."

His brother stood before him, holding out a shaking hand. The kitchen was a slaughterhouse, blood and violent death everywhere. The gathered pack stood silently, shaken to its core by the carnage. No one but Trevor dared approach him.

Mum still sobbed on the floor, bowed over Kevin's contorted carcass. Sean cradled Rhys's tortured body in his arms. There were tears everywhere Garth looked, grief and horror and sickness. He had no tears. His heart held only rage.

Why had Kevin shoved him aside like that? He'd had it under control. Now he was dead, and there was blood on Garth's hands again, all because Kevin had to take charge. Had to prove he was the alpha.

And whose fault was that? a little voice whispered. Who'd shamed the alpha in front of his whole pack?

Garth closed his eyes as a wave of self-loathing swept over him.

"Give me the knife." Trevor's face was ashen. There was a look in his eyes Garth had never seen before. Was it fear? Disgust? Why was Trevor looking at him like that?

Garth looked down, not wanting to meet that gaze. Trevor's hand was still out, palm up, waiting. Waiting for him to put something into it ... He looked down at his own hand, and saw the bloody knife. He hardly even remembered raising it. He'd been so angry, but now there was only emptiness.

He offered the knife to his brother, then changed his mind and hurled it away instead. It skittered into a corner and lay still, blood from the blade smeared obscenely across the white tiles. No one should have to touch that. No werewolf should own such a thing.

Kevin was dead. Garth tried to look, but he couldn't bear to face it straight on. His mother's grief was too immense, and his own guilt threatened to swamp him. It was Kevin's birthday, and now he was dead. Seventy years of living wiped out in a few horrific moments. A whole pack destroyed, left leaderless. His gaze found his brother's tear-streaked face. A son left without a father.

Jerry and Mac clutched each other for support on the opposite side of the circle of faces. The rest of the pack crowded into the room, shocked into silence. No one moved until Sean laid his son's body down and stood, moving as slowly as an old man. The noise of his footsteps filled the room as he crossed to the corner and picked up the stained blade.

"Pack law says the penalty for killing another wolf is death." His voice was harsh, barely above a whisper. He glared around the hushed circle, the killing knife clenched in his fist, as if daring anyone to argue.

"Or exile," Trevor said. "The penalty is death or exile, at the alpha's discretion."

The beta's hand tightened on the knife hilt until his knuckles stood out white against his tanned skin. He turned his gaze on Garth, and there was fire in those eyes.

"I'm the alpha now, and I'm going to put him down like the animal he is. He killed my son."

Garth struggled to speak, forcing his voice past the ache that spread up from his chest and throttled him. "Your son killed my father."

Trevor gave a single, broken sob. Sean didn't take his eyes off Garth.

"That was an accident." He looked around the circle. "You all saw. Rhys never meant to harm him. It was an accident."

"He took that knife," Trevor said. "He stole it from Dad's safe. He meant to kill *someone*."

For a long moment he and the beta stared at each other, testing each other out. Neither of them backed down.

"Then he has paid with his life," Sean said. "Now your brother must, too."

"No." Mum spoke for the first time, her voice raw with grief. "No more killing. I've lost my husband; I won't lose my son as well."

"It's the law," Sean said in that same emotionless tone, as if he was holding himself together by force of will. "Your mate is dead and you no longer have a voice here. It is for the new alpha to decide."

Sean had always been big on enforcing pack law, particularly if it could be done with violence. Though Trevor had long since recovered, Garth had never forgiven him for the brutality of the "lesson" he and his lackeys had meted out to Trevor that night in the clearing, when Garth had been stuck up the tree, helpless to aid his brother. He had been genuinely afraid they would kill him. He felt no fear now, though it was his own life Sean was talking about ending. He felt nothing at all.

Trevor jerked his T-shirt over his head in a violent move.

"In that case, I challenge you for leadership of this pack."

There was a collective intake of breath among the onlookers. Sean's eyes narrowed, then he handed the silver knife to Mum and began unbuttoning his shirt, slowly and deliberately.

Trevor stripped naked then stalked out into the night. The pack parted to clear his way to the back door, then followed him out. They were very quiet as they gathered on the grass underneath the gum trees. In the stillness the ghastly crunch and snap of Trevor's bones breaking and reforming echoed like gunshots.

Sean completed his own change and went to meet his rival. Garth stood next to Mum, part of a loose circle that defined the arena for the challenge. He couldn't shake the surreal feeling that this couldn't really be happening. He couldn't be standing on the grass of an ordinary suburban backyard while two great wolves circled each other warily. Behind them the clothesline loomed out of the darkness. Across the grass the waters of the pool rippled quietly, lit from below by a clear blue light. The tables by the back door were littered with glasses, many half-full, and bowls of nuts and other snacks. Above it all flapped the celebratory sign, gaily wishing *happy birthday* to a dead man. And here he stood, waiting for a fight that would decide his fate.

He glanced at Mum. Her eyes were red and puffy from crying, but her gaze never wavered from the two wolves. She had driven the silver knife into the ground at her feet and now stood guard over it, ready to hand it to whoever won this fight. It would belong to the new alpha, and with it, the power of life and death over his pack.

The two wolves were evenly matched for size. Sean had more experience, but Trevor had the advantage of youth. Trevor was dark-furred; the beta was grey except for a ruff of paler fur around his neck. Rhys had one just like it. *Had* had one.

Sean growled, his lip skinned back from his fangs, but Trevor was as silent as the shadows. They eyed one another, then Sean leapt for the younger wolf's throat. Biting and snapping, they rolled across the ground, and the circle of onlookers ebbed and flowed like the tide, trying to stay out of their way. Only his mother stood her ground, her feet planted either side of the silver knife.

There was a yelp and the two wolves parted. Blood stained the back of the white ruff, but Trevor was limping, favouring his left front leg. Sean darted in again, hoping to take advantage of the weakness, but Trevor leapt out of the way, still agile despite the injury.

They circled again, and now the limp was more pronounced. Was Trevor bunging it on to lure the other wolf into rashness? He'd still been quick when he needed to be.

Sean snarled and lunged for Trevor's throat. Their bodies went tumbling again in a vicious tangle of limbs. In the dark Garth couldn't make out more than a flash of teeth here and there.

The white-collared wolf squealed with pain and suddenly the scene froze. His brother's teeth were buried in the beta's throat and Sean lay panting on his back, showing his belly in formal submission.

The tableau held for a moment more, then Trevor released Sean and stepped back. Raising his bloody muzzle to the sky, he howled his victory. The neighbourhood dogs burst into a frenzy of barking, but in the dark backyard all the wolves lowered their heads before their new alpha.

His mother bent to retrieve the knife as the two shifted back to human form. Sean lay naked and bleeding on the grass, but Trevor ignored him. He accepted the ritual knife then turned to Garth.

"As leader of this pack I declare you exiled, from this and every gathering of wolves." There was no mercy in his face. "No pack may offer you aid or shelter. From this day forward, you are condemned to live alone."

A wolf's worst nightmare. What was a wolf without his pack? He met his brother's eyes and nodded, not trusting himself to speak. Trevor had just risked his own life to save Garth's, but that was all he could do.

A lone wolf again. Even he, the eternal outsider, hadn't been able to make that work before. The taste of the pig hunter's flesh in his mouth still haunted him. He turned to his mother. Her eyes brimmed with tears again as she took him in a fierce hug.

"Take care of yourself," she whispered into his shirt, and then she let him go and he was on his own. No one else said a word, not Trevor, not even Jerry, her face drained of all colour beneath the bright purple hair. He glanced at Carly but she looked away, unwilling even to look at him now. He was a leper. Unclean. Every face was carved of stone, turned against him or turned away.

He left his father's seventieth birthday party and drove away without looking back.

ONE HUNDRED AND NINETY-FIFTH MOON
Fifteen years a werewolf

He'd gone back to Melbourne, but Avery had made it quite clear that he wouldn't share his territory with an exile, so he'd left his job and moved to an ugly town on a windy, godforsaken stretch of the coast. Its main attraction was that there wasn't a werewolf pack for two hundred kilometres. He got a job at the local supermarket, and spent his first two weeks fortifying the cellar of the house he'd rented, building a prison even his wolf couldn't break out of come full moon. He didn't trust himself to run free under the moon without the control of an alpha.

He'd been there two months, and was facing the prospect of his third full moon locked in a concrete cell with only a slab of steak for company, when he received a call.

"Hey. It's me," said his brother's voice.

He sucked in a shaky breath. He hadn't had any contact with Trevor since he'd walked out of that fatal birthday party. "Hi" didn't seem to cover it, but he couldn't think of anything else to say.

"Umm … hi? Are you allowed to talk to me?"

"Sure I am. You're still my brother."

Tears stung at his eyes, and he blinked them away. Damn, but it was good to hear him say that. He'd been so afraid his brother would never forgive him for Kevin's death.

"How—how's Mum?"

Trevor sighed. "Not so good. She's still pretty cut up about Dad. Worried about you, too. How are you?"

"I'm fine." He had a sudden memory of Deb, all those years ago, sitting at the dining table telling him she was *fine*, in that clipped way that meant she was anything but.

"Really?" It sounded like Trevor didn't believe him any more than Garth had believed Deb. "Where are you living? What are you doing at full moon? Have you got somewhere to run?"

"I'm living in the armpit of the universe, and I don't run. I've built myself a cage."

There was a sharp intake of breath on the other end of the line. "A cage? That's no way to live."

"No," he agreed sadly. "It's not."

But what else could he do? He couldn't trust himself to run loose on his own. There were not going to be any more pig hunters in his future. If he had to sit in a cage every full moon, then so be it. It was probably no more than he deserved, anyway.

Maybe Trevor should have let Sean kill him.

"Listen," said his brother. "I've been thinking. Have you heard a proving's started?"

"No." He hadn't had any contact with anyone from the shifter community since he'd moved. Not much contact with anyone at all, in fact. He went to work and came home again, and that was about it. He wasn't exactly in the partying mood lately; he was still processing Kevin's death. Rhys's he couldn't care less about; someone should have put that jerk down years ago. But Kevin's death weighed on his conscience something fierce. "Where? Here in Australia?"

Not that he was particularly interested, but Trevor seemed to require a response.

"Yes. Elizabeth presented the candidates to the domain last week."

Elizabeth was the dragon queen of this domain, which included all of Australia, among other places. He didn't know much about dragon business—he preferred to avoid them wherever possible—but he did know that when a queen neared the end of her life, her daughters engaged in a fight to the death called a proving. Last woman standing got the throne after mummy died.

"And?" He presumed his brother was telling him this for a reason.

"And one of them's dead already. Blown up in the middle of the Presentation Ball."

"Were you there?"

"Yep. Elizabeth was mightily pissed. So now there's only four daughters left, and they're all running scared."

"Why are you getting involved?"

"It's kind of hard not to. You know what dragons are like—they don't take no for an answer. All you can really do is pick one to support and hope you backed a winner."

"Sounds dangerous."

"Yeah, well, werewolves are pretty small fry in the shifter world. I figure the pack's pretty safe. Anyway, I've done some work for one of them, Leandra, and now she's looking to beef up her security team, and I thought of you."

Really? Being a bouncer at a nightclub hardly qualified him to work as a bodyguard for someone three other people were actively trying to kill.

"What's she like?"

"She's a dragon—she's a bitch. But she treats her people well and she's got some great guys on her team. Her security chief's a wyvern called Lucinda Chan. Heard of her?"

"No."

"I think you'd like her. I told her about you and she seemed keen." Trevor hesitated. "I know it's not the same as a pack, but it's got to be better than sitting alone in a cage."

Just about anything would be. He was touched that his brother had gone to this trouble for him. He would be a good alpha.

"Okay. I'll do it."

"Great! I've already arranged an interview for you with Luce. And Garth? Try not to stuff it up."

***

The car wound down a long road between towering gums, into a kind of natural bowl in the landscape that sat nestled among tree-covered ridges. He hadn't passed a house in some time, or anything that even hinted that humans had ever set foot there. At the end of the long road he found a driveway, blocked by heavy wrought-iron gates. The olde worlde look was offset by a very modern camera mounted beside the gate, above an intercom.

He pressed the button.

"Yes?" said a man's voice.

"Garth Maclaren," he said. "Ms Chan is expecting me."

The man didn't reply, but the gates swung open and Garth drove in.

The place looked like something off a film set: *billionaire's country estate, set on rolling green lawns.* The house was white, with many large windows and French doors. Not the most secure, though the view was probably pretty. Maybe they had magical defences he couldn't see. The central part of the house was two-storey, with a long single-storey wing stretching out on either side. He wondered how many people lived here.

Ahead of him the driveway divided, with one part sweeping up to the front of the house, and the other disappearing around the side of one of the wings, presumably to a garage around the back. He parked out front.

A knocker in the shape of a dragon's head adorned the heavy wooden door, which opened before he could raise his hand. An enormous man stood there, Polynesian or Maori by the look of him. Garth rarely felt small, but this guy could have made two of him. He stepped aside, unsmiling, to allow Garth to enter.

"Weapons?" he asked.

"No." Back in Melbourne he'd been in the habit of carrying a knife. Not all of Avery's business ventures were entirely above board, and some days Garth had been glad of it. But bringing a knife to a job interview seemed like making the wrong kind of impression.

"Arms out, please." The big guy wasn't taking his word for it. He frisked Garth efficiently then led him through the enormous marble foyer, past the sweeping staircase, and down a long corridor. He knocked on a door then opened it without waiting for a reply.

"Here's the werewolf guy, Luce."

Garth followed him in and found a small Chinese woman seated behind an L-shaped desk that held an array of computers. One of those massive windows showed a view of the front lawn. She'd probably watched him drive in.

"Sit." She gestured to one of two chairs in front of the desk. He sat obediently, and the big Maori guy took up a position by the closed door. Having someone looming behind him made his skin crawl, but he tried to ignore it and focus on the Chinese woman.

Lucinda Chan. Trevor hadn't said much about her, other than that she was a wyvern and the head of Leandra's security team. Wyverns were pretty high up the shifter food chain, but in her human form she didn't seem that impressive. She looked as though Garth could snap her in two without even trying.

"Your brother recommended you." She spoke without a trace of an accent. "Did he tell you what happened at the Presentation Ball?"

"Yes."

"My mistress is very keen to recruit additional security after the incident. Loyalty will be richly rewarded."

His mouth fell open as she named a salary. She was talking serious money.

"However, the dangers are very real." Her expression never changed as she spoke, as if she were some beautiful emotionless doll. "There are three dragons out there who want my mistress dead. Your job will be to make sure they don't succeed. I can't guarantee that you'll live to a ripe old age."

He shrugged. "I'm not afraid of dying."

One finger tapped on the desk top as she regarded him thoughtfully. "Have you ever killed anyone before this recent unpleasantness with your pack?"

Unpleasantness? Was that what it was? Lord, she was a cool customer.

"Yes." He was glad she didn't ask for details.

"Are you any good with a gun?"

"I'm a decent shot but I prefer knives."

She continued to pepper him with questions, some personal: *have you got a family? no? a girlfriend?* Others were more perplexing. Why did she care how much he weighed? At the end she stood abruptly and told him to follow.

Standing, she barely came up to his armpit. Next to her, even his mother would look tall. He followed her, with the big Maori guy bringing up the rear. She led him out the back of the house. There were several freestanding buildings here: a couple of small cottages, a garage big enough to house a whole fleet of cars, a building whose glass walls were slightly steamed by the heated pool inside, and a large stables complex.

His nose told him that many horses had once called the stables home, but that they were currently empty. Luce hauled open the big sliding door on a huge barn and led him inside. It was dark after the bright sunshine outside, especially after his large shadow slid the door shut again. The massive space was mainly empty, lit only by a row of high, slightly dusty windows along the back wall. A few exercise machines were arranged along one side, and a large space in the centre was covered with floor mats such as you'd find in a martial arts school.

Luce stopped in the centre of the mats and turned to face him.

"Hit me."

He stepped onto the mats. Hit her? She was half his size.

"Do you have a problem with taking orders from a woman?" she asked when he made no move. "Hit me."

He glanced back at the huge bodyguard. Hitting *him* would be a fairer contest. But if it was what she wanted …

He threw a punch.

The next thing he knew he was flat on his back on the mats, staring up into the dark recesses of the roof. Gasping for air. It happened so fast he didn't even know how he'd got there.

The big Maori guy chuckled. "The same thing happened to me the first time, too."

"You a shifter?" He scrambled to his feet, feeling like an idiot. At least the guy's smile was sympathetic.

"Nope. Hundred per cent human."

Well, that just made it worse. Shifters had faster reflexes. Wyvern or not, someone the size of an undernourished twelve-year-old shouldn't have been able to lay Garth out on the mat.

The undernourished twelve-year-old smiled, the first hint of emotion he'd seen from her. "Would you like to try that with a little more commitment this time?"

You bet he would. He rolled his shoulders, loosening his neck, and approached her cautiously. She watched him come, her body in a relaxed stance.

He drove a hard right at her face, followed by a lightning blow to her solar plexus with his left. Except it wasn't there, and he was on his back again.

He sprang to his feet, properly riled now. Five humiliating minutes followed, in which he only landed one glancing blow, and hit the deck more times than he could count. Meanwhile Luce hardly seemed to move. She barely even raised a sweat.

Slow clapping brought the farce to an end. He spun around, fighting for air, and saw that a blonde woman in a white bikini had come in while he was getting acquainted with the mats. She had a towel slung over one shoulder, and an amused expression on her face.

"He hit you once," she said to Luce. "You must be slipping."

"He's got shifter reflexes, and he's fitter than most," his tiny nemesis replied.

The blonde woman ran her gaze up and down his sweat-soaked body as if she were evaluating a steer at market. "So I see." Finally her cool blue eyes settled on his face. "You must be Trevor's brother. You're taller than I was expecting."

"Trevor's the runt of the litter."

A smile twitched at the corner of her mouth, and she turned to Luce. "I like him. Have one of the thralls show him around."

Then she sauntered out.

"That was Leandra?" Who else would be throwing orders around here like that?

"Yes," said Luce.

His new boss. The woman who could one day rule the whole domain—as long as he managed to keep her alive.

"What do you think her chances are of winning the proving?"

"That's up to us, isn't it?" Luce held out her hand and he took it, feeling the hard callouses there. She was a lot tougher than she looked, as he'd just discovered. Hopefully Leandra would prove the same. They shook hands. "Well done."

He was surprised at how much the simple praise meant, coming from her.

"Yeah, good job, bro." The big Maori came forward, enveloping Garth's hand in his enormous meaty one and shaking enthusiastically.

"Does this mean I've got the job?"

Luce smiled, and it was like the sun coming out from behind the clouds. "Welcome to the team."

The team. He liked the sound of that. Somewhere to belong, with people who didn't judge him based on his birth. Somewhere he could make a difference.

"Bring it on," he said.

THE END

Thank you for reading! If you enjoyed *Moonborn*, please take a moment to leave a short review. Your feedback helps other readers find the book, and I would be very grateful for your assistance in helping to spread the word.

Sign up to my newsletter for updates on new releases, plus special deals and book news.

Sign up by visiting my website, www.marinafinlayson.com.

If you enjoyed this novella, don't miss The Proving trilogy, which picks up the story where *Moonborn* ends.

Book 1: *Twiceborn*
Book 2: *The Twiceborn Queen*
Book 3: *Twiceborn Endgame*

ACKNOWLEDGEMENTS

This time I only have one beta reader to thank: my darling husband, who is also my biggest cheerleader. But that's not the end of the thank-yous! Thanks also to Shayne for the gorgeous cover, and a big fat *merci beaucoup* to Tammi for her superb editing, even though we may never agree on ellipses.

ABOUT THE AUTHOR

Marina Finlayson is a reformed wedding organist who now writes fantasy. She is married and shares her Sydney home with three kids, a large collection of dragon statues and one very stupid dog with a death wish.

She is the author of The Proving trilogy: *Twiceborn, The Twiceborn Queen* and *Twiceborn Endgame*.

9 780099 423913 6